FEB 2022

WITHDRAWN

Running on Empty

AWARD-WINNING AUTHOR

RUTH LOGAN HERNE

Mount Laurel Library
100 Walt Whitman Avenue
Mount Laurel, NJ 08054-9539
856-234-7319
www.mountlaurellibrary.org

Copyright © 2013 by Ruth Logan Herne

All rights reserved under International and Pan-American Copyright Conventions

By payment of required fees, you have been granted the *non*-exclusive, *non*-transferable right to access and read the text of this book. No part of this text may be reproduced, transmitted, downloaded, decompiled, reverse engineered, or stored in or introduced into any information storage and retrieval system, in any form or by any means, whether electronic or mechanical, now known or hereinafter invented without the express written permission of copyright owner.

Please Note

The reverse engineering, uploading, and/or distributing of this book via the internet or via any other means without the permission of the copyright owner is illegal and punishable by law. Please purchase only authorized electronic editions, and do not participate in or encourage electronic piracy of copyrighted materials. Your support of the author's rights is appreciated

No part of this book may be reproduced or transmitted in any form or by any electronic or mechanical means, including photocopying, recording or by any information storage and retrieval system, without the written permission of the publisher, except where permitted by law.

Thank you.

Cover design by The Killion Group
Interior format by The Killion Group
http://thekilliongroupinc.com

DEDICATION

For Beth, my "first" editor, my beautiful daughter whose love and support have helped me establish this writing career. I love you!

ACKNOWLEDGEMENTS

A huge thank you to the good folks from Canton and Potsdam, New York, whose advice and encouragement helped me create "North Country" stories. To my daughter-in-law Karen Blodgett, a runner whose prowess amazes me. Thanks to Dave for his advice on hunting and fishing, to Nancy for the time she spent advising me about North Country protocol. I learned to never go up a driveway with a "No Trespassing" sign! And to the Ostranders for their hospitality and counsel on people, sheep and living up north. This writer is grateful!

CHAPTER ONE

"So. She's back, huh?"

Chief of Police Joe McIntyre refused to look up as Officer Kim Riccitti strode into the office. Eyes down, he scanned a report as if it were any old day. Shifting his chair, he reached for the electric pencil sharpener. The discount model ground noisily as he sharpened the guaranteed-not-to-break pencil with more pressure than needed. The tiny but audible *snap*! belied the manufacturer's claim. Joe swallowed a sigh, worked his jaw and kept his gaze flat. "I heard."

Kim looked his way. "And?"

"The updated lecture schedule is on your desk." His tone left no room for discussion. Kim would help him counsel incoming students for four northern New York universities on blue-light programs and self-defense maneuvers. In cooperation with the county sheriff's department, they shared a weekly program throughout the fall to fortify new coeds. Sometimes the older ones. All were welcome.

"Orientation week is a killer," Kim grumbled, grabbing fresh coffee, her movements sure. "You going to see her?"

Joe swerved. The muscle in his cheek twitched a warning. He jerked his head toward her cube. “We’ve got work, Kim.”

Her look of surprise made him wish he could snatch the words back. Too late. Eyes narrowed, she shrugged and nodded as she moved to the gray metal desk dominating her workspace around the corner. “I’m on it, Chief.”

Swiveling back, Joe punched keys with more force than needed, watching new figures take place in Forest Hills history.

The numbers looked good. Violent crimes were nonexistent in the town proper. St. Lawrence County’s proximity to the Canadian border kept life interesting for the sheriff’s office with the elevated terrorist levels, but in Forest Hills, New York, college brawls, neighbor disputes and marital conflicts were the biggies.

And Emil Richter, the town drunk. Right out of Mayberry he was, unafraid to nab a cell on nights when drowning his sorrows left him too wired to make the drive home.

But that was okay. A seven-person police force had no desire to rub elbows with the violent crimes unit of the sheriff’s department.

Joe worked to keep his mind on the report in his hands, shoving the news of the day aside. News he’d heard thrice over. First his mother called, then a friend. Now Kim. All anxious to console him.

Consolation was the last thing he needed. Anger management would be a better choice. The idea that he could come face-to-face with his ex-wife all these years later had his fingers clenching.

He bottled the surge of anger. Police work had no tolerance for reprisal, no matter how just it seemed. Nor did his faith. But the rush of feelings vying for recognition inside him brought no comfort.

Kim's drone reminded him she was an auditory learner, able to recall her presentation better once she practiced out loud.

He was the opposite. Once read, information stayed locked in his brain, affording him an easy time in school. Too easy, his mother had affirmed. But he'd had plenty of time for sports and girls as a result.

One girl, actually.

Again he shoved the thought away, angry that the simple mention of her presence brought everything back. Deciding to walk the town center to expend nervous energy, he stood, grabbed his cap, started to put it on and turned as the entry bell jangled.

Annie.

His heart paused. So did his hands, raised up, over his head as he set the cap in place. For a second he was a statue, stern and immovable, his eyes on hers. She gulped, her hand gripping the inside knob as if guarding an escape route. She swallowed again.

"I heard you were back." Joe kept his voice flat. He tugged the officer's cap into place, eyeing her.

She nodded, took a breath, then eased down the steps to the desk, her eyes on his. "I knew you'd hear."

Her voice was soft. Not as lyrical as it used to be. Long and lean, she still had a runner's build. She took a deeper breath and exhaled on a half-sigh. "I didn't want us to meet in the Family Dollar or something. I thought..."

Her hand fluttered. Her voice trailed off. She broke from the intensity of his look and glanced around his office. "This is nice, Joe."

Nice? *Nice?* She had the audacity to come in here after years of silence, look around his well-run, carefully orchestrated law enforcement office and call it nice? His resentment climbed. He'd give her nice.

Swallowing words, he stayed silent. Motionless. Making things as uncomfortable for her as he could without breaching the letter of the law.

Her look flitted to him. For a brief second he saw something that almost pierced his armor. Regret? She swiped slim fingers against the sides of her thighs. *Good*, he thought. *Let her sweat.* His silence unnerved her, and he had no intention of doing anything to make this easier. He kept his look impassive. Distant.

Cold.

"My mother isn't well." She moved to the window where Venetian blinds allowed him to adjust light. She fiddled with the cord, the morning sun casting a sheen of gold against straight, brown hair, curved at the ends. For a moment he wondered if those locks were as soft as he remembered. Silk-soft, smelling of spiced vanilla.

Annie took a step, jerking his thoughts back.

"I know this is awkward," she explained. "I'm sorry about that. I had no choice." She lifted narrow shoulders in a slight shrug. "She's my mother," she added, as if that clarified everything.

But then, Annie wasn't too good at offering explanation. Like why she'd run out after six months of marriage, leaving him with nothing but a scribbled note, wounded pride and empty dresser drawers. For a long time, every hint of light and joy had gone with her.

His muscles bunched. He ignored the tremor, refusing to revisit the scene of that silent apartment. Time had healed him.

Well, hardened him, anyway. He'd have to forgive to heal, and he had no intention of doing that. Not without bowing and scraping on her part, none of which seemed forthcoming. She crossed back to his desk, put her hands on the scarred cherry surface, and met his gaze. "I'll try not to get in your way, Joe. Are you still going to Holy Trinity?"

He nodded, keeping his eyes void of emotion. They'd been married in that church. She'd come down the aisle in her simple white gown and he was sure he'd never seen anything more beautiful. The look of love and trust she'd offered him that day - where had it gone in six short months?

"All right. I'll take Mom and—" she missed a beat, then continued, "to Westside Community. She hasn't been able to go for a while."

Guilt stabbed Joe. He'd heard that Maura was unwell, but hadn't done what he would have for anyone else. Check on her, bring her little treats. Show her some small-town caring. He'd ignored the situation, which was tricky since he owned the house she lived in, a modest rental left by his grandmother. He and his brother each inherited two properties. A nice nest egg for a pair of single guys. As chance would have it, Twelve-forty-one Old Orchard Road was one of his.

The home of Maura Kellwyn.

He received a monthly reminder, like it or not. A check, signed with her weakening script.

He seldom went there. She rarely complained about conditions, so he avoided examining them, and when she did need something done, he commissioned his brother to fix it. But as a court officer, he should have made sure she was all right, and he hadn't. He shelved the feeling, wanting nothing to do with a past he'd kept masked until today.

Annie moved to the door, tentative. One hand came up, spreading her hair back in a gesture he remembered like yesterday. She performed that same ritual after every race, searching the crowd for him while the right hand smoothed flyaway hairs from her eyes, her cheeks.

Cheeks that looked as fair and smooth as they had eight years before. He bit back the anger threatening to choke him.

"Good-bye, Joe." The door jangled again as she stepped out. For a few seconds, sunshine streamed in, flooding the entry with bright, summer light.

Then it darkened again as the door swung shut. Through the tilted blinds he saw her head north, toward the shopping district, her gait graceful.

He strode to the door and closed the blinds, shutting out any vestige of August sun. Advising Kim of his intent, he walked out the door, shoulders back, head high, as if he hadn't a care in the world.

Annie had turned north when she left the building.

Joe turned south.

CHAPTER TWO

Anne's heart slowed as she passed the aged brick library. *Not bad*, she congratulated herself. *Less than a quarter-mile to resume normal sinus rhythm. Now, if my hands would stop quivering, my knees stop shaking...*

You there, God? She glanced heavenward. *Me, again. How come I didn't realize the emotional jab would have a physiological punch? My gut hurts, my throat's sore, and my heart's out of control. Do you think Forest Hills has stocked up on portable defibrillators?*

Glancing around, she noted the run-down condition of the town center. Empty storefronts dotted the main drag. Heaved sidewalks screamed of long, cold winters. Faded flags hung limp in the summer sun. Taking it all in, she shook her head. *Not likely,* she mused, the buzz abating. *Probably best to avoid the heart attack if at all possible. But the look on Joe's face—*

Eyes trained ahead, Anne ignored the glances cast her way. She sensed her presence inspired more than one conversation.

But wasn't that why she'd come to town without her mother or son? So people would see her, speculate; get it out of their systems before the rest of the family bore the brunt of conjecture. It seemed a sensible solution, but right now she waxed sympathetic to every goldfish she'd ever ogled. Life in a clear glass bowl was no picnic.

In the store she grabbed a cart, hoping no one read her inner battle. She'd perfected the maneuver years ago, presenting a face that didn't reflect the humiliation teeming within. It seemed like nothing to pull the old Anne out and dust the façade off. Like dirty dishwater newly released, years of pricey therapy gurgled down the drain. For a moment she was transported, the vintage grocery reducing her to childhood status.

"Look who we have here." A familiar voice dripped honey, insincere. "Annie McIntyre. How long has it been?" The bleached blond eyed Anne from behind the deli counter. The thick scent of smoked meat and ripe cheese drifted like a fresh-made hoagie. "Ten years, give or take?"

Anne refused to acknowledge the time frame or correct the name. She'd been Anne since leaving town eight years before. Once the divorce was final, she'd reassumed Kellwyn as her last name. Leaning into the cart, she offered a smile, a logical first step. "Hello, Corrine."

"I expect you're back because your mama's strugglin'," the other woman supposed, her gaze pit-bull tough, as if sizing Anne up and finding her lacking. The in-your-face attitude was no more than Anne expected, so why did it hurt this much? *Never let them see you sweat...* That phrase shaped her running career in high school and college.

It helped now, too. "She needs a hand," Anne agreed, reaching for a pound of fine-grained pasta.

"There's cheaper stuff 'round the corner," Corrine advised. "When you're on a budget, every penny counts."

Since Anne was reasonably sure Corrine had no intimate knowledge of her cash flow, she added another box of the pricey pasta for effect. "This will do.

And I see Abe's got fresh artichokes over there." She looked past the deli to the L-shaped produce corner and moved that way. "Perfect."

Abe Shofeld had run this grocery for forty years. Appearances said he hadn't given much thought to modernization. Decades-old fluorescent lights buzzed their discontent while displays bore a Pleasantville aura. Everything neat, stacked in perfect succession, can by can, sack by sack. She thought of the super centers she'd utilized and sighed.

In the North Country, not much changed.

Forest Hills locals shopped the old grocery, accustomed to the narrow aisles and quaint lighting. Cash registers manufactured before scanners and UPCs were considered. Frozen food cases with fogged windows. Tough times and few manufacturing jobs forced people to move, businesses to close, leaving little recourse to those remaining.

Moving down the first aisle, Anne glared at the prices. Twice what she'd pay at a wholesale club. She bit back a sigh. For the moment, she had enough money to take care of food and her mother's bills, thanks to her mother's Social Security check and Anne's frugality. As things progressed, she'd help in whatever way necessary. That's what daughters did, right? The good ones, anyway. The ones that didn't—

She pushed that aside, along with the anchor of guilt that grew heavier as she'd cruised north on I-81. Her mother needed help because of her declining health. Anne loved her mother. Simple equation for a high school math teacher.

She just wished it wasn't here. Forest Hills held too many thoughts that jumbled, confusing her. Reminding her of so many bad choices.

But she was grown up now. Fully functional. At least that's what her Georgia counselor promised. Turning left, another familiar voice greeted her.

"Anne. How are you? Pretty as ever, I see." Sally Mort, Anne's high school science teacher, stepped her way as Anne moved toward the cashiers.

Anne smiled. "I'm fine, thank you. How can it be twelve years since biology class and you haven't changed a bit?"

The older woman laughed. "Oh, plenty's changed, my dear. The mirror tells me that. But your years have been kind. You still shine in a way that makes heads turn."

Heat suffused Anne's cheeks. Back in the day, she'd grown accustomed to compliments. Her running had led to three state titles and a regional first place in the Foot Locker Cross Country Invitational held at Van Cortlandt Park in the Bronx. She always made it a point to stop at the bakery across from that racecourse, carting home the sumptuous carrot cake sold there. Or nut tarts. Something wonderful to carry back to her mother. Lack of funds kept Maura home, working, while Anne ran more distant races. Her mother lived a life of sacrifice for her one child, and how had Anne repaid the favor?

She hadn't.

"Thank you." She smiled at the teacher who inspired her own certification. A moment of silence made Anne wonder if other shoppers had tuned into their conversation. As if Abe had secret cameras and mikes furtively placed to enhance the gossip factor.

Mrs. Mort touched her arm, smiled, and headed toward the registers, chatting easily. "So. Tell me what you're doing now. Besides helping your mother, that is."

Did everyone know why she returned? She'd arrived less than forty-eight hours ago. The speed of informational transmission was impressive, even for Forest Hills. She didn't sigh. Instead she mustered a smile at this gesture of friendship. "Mom does need help," she admitted. "I teach," she continued, noting her old teacher's look of pleased surprise. "Science and math. You were good inspiration, Mrs. Mort."

"Music to my ears, Anne, and I'm sure you're wonderful," the older woman declared. "Will you be working here? I know there's a junior high math opening." Her gaze thoughtful, she tapped her chin with a teacher-like finger. "One of the staff just got called up to his reserve unit. They're interviewing for one at the high school level as well."

Anne froze. The thought of working at Forest Hills High School, the school she'd represented as a runner, chilled her. The district that still championed Tom Baldwin as coach of the year. Dear God...

No. That couldn't happen. Not in this lifetime. She shook her head, keeping her tone light. "I don't know how long I'll be here," she hedged. "It all depends on my mother's health." Narrowing her eyes, she gave a little shrug. "And work. I figured I'd look for something part time so I wouldn't have to leave her all day."

"Hmm." Sally nodded. "Understandable. Well, there's always required tutoring. Pays fifteen dollars an hour and you set your own hours. You can schedule the students on an after-hours basis at school or the child's home. You'll need the number." Reaching into a well-organized purse, she scribbled digits on a Post-It and handed Anne the yellow square. "Central Office. Give them a call. There are plenty of kids who could use your expertise to prepare them for the tougher Regents' examinations. No benefits, though."

Anne nodded her thanks and tucked the number away. "I appreciate this, Mrs. Mort."

"We're all grown up now." The older woman laughed before giving the younger teacher a quick hug. "Call me Sally. We're colleagues."

Anne made a face of reluctance. "I don't know if I can," she confessed. "The thought of calling my old teachers by their first names intimidates me."

"You'll get used to it." Sally's voice and face offered easy support. She gave Anne's arm a light touch. "It *is* good to have you back here, dear. You've been missed."

Anne's smile slipped. Her heart stutter-stepped, recalling the scattered looks she'd gotten on the walk over. "That's nice to hear."

Her voice smacked doubt at the assertion. She was pretty certain that few had missed her once she'd left Joe. Forest Hills kept its successful children close to the heart. She'd managed to break one of those hearts.

Sally gave her arm a reassuring squeeze. "It all works out, Anne. When life pushes us forward, God covers our backs, one way or another."

Did he? She hoped so. It sure hadn't felt like anyone had her back when she'd come face to face with Joe, his blue eyes searing into her soul. Almost as if he saw what she was. What she'd been. What she'd done those first years away.

Impossible. Joe would never track me through police channels like a common criminal. Would he?

Nixing the thought, she accepted the hug Sally offered, but fought tears when the older woman whispered, "Welcome home, Anne."

Once she checked out, Anne lugged the bags back to her car, parked in the faded municipal lot across from the police station. Popping the trunk, she stowed her packages, trying not to picture Joe inside the building. The red brick exterior could use a good cleaning, but the diminished Adirondack work force meant less tax money all around. Shabby exteriors and covered shop windows told a silent tale of woe.

The police station windows gleamed, though. That would be Joe's doing. He'd always done the windows in their apartment, repeating his Granny's proclamation that windows were a light unto the soul. As such, they should be kept polished, letting God's light in. She'd laughed at the sweetness of the story eight years ago, but carried the tradition with her. In both Florida and

Georgia, Anne Kellwyn's windows had shimmered. She couldn't say the same about her soul.

A tug of pressure at the back of her neck made Anne stiffen. She felt eyes, staring. With concerted effort, she refused to turn, not wanting to know who watched. Was it Leila from the hair salon, or Boog from the wood shop? Forest Hills was small town, U.S.A., and until they got used to seeing her again, she'd be gossip fodder. So be it. Swinging open the door of her Honda, she glanced at the municipal office building once more.

Joe.

He stood still and distinct, the rugged planes of his face firm and structured, his blue-black hair cut short with just a hint of rampant curl. Eyes as blue as the August sky above.

Anger and disgust. They emanated from him, constricting her heart under the combined pressure. It was there in the cool, hard look of assessment. His posture. The way his nostrils flared. Eight years of unexplained absence had been torture for him. Why hadn't she realized how much? Was she that lost in herself? That selfish?

She faced him square, refusing to hide her eyes or duck her head, determined to stand her ground.

Except...

She couldn't. Not in the face of his scorn, his righteous anger. Well-deserved anger, at that.

If only...

There were no 'ifs'. Not anymore. Not for a very long time. Unable to handle the intensity, Anne ducked into her car, started the engine, and headed down Route 11, wondering why she thought seeing Joe would clear the air.

It hadn't happened, and likely wouldn't, not when a four-minute meeting destroyed years of careful avoidance.

And why did he look so good after all this time? Shouldn't he have a spreading middle? Hair loss?

Sagging jowls? Instead, his rugged good looks had ripened, making the police chief a better edition of the sheriff's deputy she'd fallen in love with years ago.

Not fair...

But then, Anne had figured that out long ago. Justice didn't necessarily factor into life's equations. She loved the principles of mathematics for that reason. Math problems had one correct answer. No shades of gray, no subjectivity, no maybes obscuring the edges of right and wrong, and if you missed one question, it had no residual effect on the remainder of the test.

No so in life. It only took one mistake to undermine a future of happiness, a chance for the happily-ever-after she'd longed for as a child.

She'd had it for a brief time. The joy, the love, the ardent appreciation of a wonderful man, his love a cloak of protection and solace. But when past sins tripped her up, even Joe's love wasn't enough to shield her.

Instead, she'd run as far and fast as she could, losing everything she'd ever hoped to find.

CHAPTER THREE

"Mommy!" Kyle raced out of the house, the wooden screen door slapping shut behind him. "I'm glad you're back. Grammy said I could have ice cream if I was good while you were gone."

"Were you?" Anne smiled, handing off a lightweight bag to the nearly six-year-old boy.

He nodded, earnest. "I was super-good. I carried the wash out and handed it to her."

Anne sent her mother a scolding look as she stepped through the entry. Tilting her chin toward the hanging laundry, she shook her head. "You could have used the dryer," she reminded the aging woman. "Less work."

"The few months we get of nice weather are held in high regard," her mother retorted. "You're back north now." She raised an arch look to Anne. "Warmth is transient up here."

Too true. "I remember putting in some long, cold miles on these highways mid-winter," Anne agreed. "But you could have waited, Mom. I'd have hung them for you."

Her mother patted Kyle's shoulder. "This way Kyle and I worked together. We make a good team, if I do say so myself."

The boy beamed. Anne smiled. Her mother's attitude softened where Kyle was concerned. She loved the boy, his innocence and vitality.

The circumstances of his birth? A whole different story.

"You do make a good team." Anne shifted her look to her son. "Hey, Kyle, bring around the rest of those packages, will you?" When he groaned, she raised a motherly brow. "Your trip to the movies depends on a cooperative attitude."

His countenance brightened. She nodded in satisfaction as he headed for the door. "Much better." Once the door smacked shut, she turned back to her mother. "I think I'll make a trip to Watertown and lay in supplies from the wholesale club. The prices in town are awful."

Maura nodded. "They inflated them as more and more businesses bellied-up. Fewer customers meant higher prices for the ones remaining. They're not so bad in Canton and Potsdam, though."

"Because there's no economic logic in that," offered Anne practically. "Higher prices make it worth people's time to drive farther."

"Makes sense," agreed Maura.

"Kyle and I will make the trip this week," Anne continued. "Feel up to coming?" She issued the invitation knowing her mother's health made shopping difficult, but wanting her to feel welcome.

Maura considered the offer, then shook her head. "I get too out of breath. But getting into town, going to church?" Her voice heartened. "That I'll do. Reverend Wilson sends me prayer booklets and stops to see me regular. He's a good man." Settling into her chair, she picked up her knitting. "Tight with God. Not afraid to issue a challenge. Expect goodness."

Was that a body slam or a casual observation? Anne paused, unsure. Deciding to ignore the comment, she thought of what she'd said to Joe about going to a different church. She sounded her mother out. "Have you ever gone to Westside Community?"

Her mother snorted. "Why would I? Pastor Wilson is the man for me. When he talks God's word, I listen."

Anne thought hard. Maybe they could attend separate services. Turning, she asked, "Do they still have two services?"

Maura shook her head. "No need, now. The college kids don't come and the community is smaller than when you left." Anne didn't miss her mother's note of resignation. "Back then, we built those extra classrooms to handle the influx of students. Remember that, Annie?

Anne nodded. The new wing had been a source of pride and joy for the local community, a step up educationally.

"Now they're science rooms. Labs. Resource areas." She sighed, her eyes intent on her handiwork. "No one stays here anymore. They spread their wings and take off to see the world. Not much to offer hereabouts unless you're a farmer or storekeeper. Or a teacher."

Anne refused to take the comments personally. She'd noted the decline in housing. Homes dulled by forces of nature, yards untended, peeling finishes. When money became scarce, amenities like paint and shutters went by the wayside. She addressed her mother's last comment. "I saw Sally Mort in town. She gave me the card for Central Office, in case I want to tutor."

"You need a job, Anne, if you insist on staying," admonished her mother. Anne sent her a warning look as Kyle banged in the door. Waiting until the boy scurried back out, Maura continued, "The visiting nurse will come by regular. They'll give me a home health aide too, at least part time. You need insurance for you and Kyle. Tutoring won't get you that, and you'd spend your paycheck on an out-of-pocket expense you shouldn't have. Over nine hundred dollars a month for something you'd get free by working at school. It makes no sense."

Anne opened her mouth, but Maura held up a quieting hand. "Think about it. Please." The soft click of knitting needles punctuated the remark, her unsteady hands slow but methodical. "I'd feel better knowing you and Kyle are covered. He'll be in school, you could teach and I wouldn't feel so dependent."

The last comment explained so much.

Anne knew her mother. She understood Maura's fierce sense of honor. It wasn't easy to come full circle in life. To give up your autonomy, let your children take the reins.

And she was right. Lack of health insurance could wipe out Anne's savings with one small mishap. She met her mother's eye. "I'll send out my portfolio. See what's available. Canton or Potsdam might have something open. Maybe Redmond." She sank into the comforting softness of her mother's old sofa. "You're right about the insurance stuff, Mom. And the independence. I know it's a bitter pill."

Her mother lowered her chin at Anne's attempt to understand. "I like things my way."

"And that's difficult now," Anne acknowledged. She smiled as Kyle carried in the last sack. He deposited the bag, and hustled off to wage Jurassic-war along the worn front porch. "He's gotten big, hasn't he? I think he's built like Dad."

Maura nodded, her eyes softening. "Wide shoulders, deep chest. He certainly didn't take after you."

"Except his eyes," Anne corrected. Kyle had inherited her amber eyes with flecks of brown and an almost gray rim around the iris. Hazel, some said. Whatever that was.

When she was a kid, a class bully called them mutant eyes. Wondered out loud if she was an alien. Hearing her classmates laugh, she'd felt like an alien until Joe McIntyre bloodied the other boy's nose for picking on her. Making her cry.

From that moment on, Joe championed her. He became the big brother she never had until the time came when he was no longer satisfied with a sibling-like role. Then he came around in earnest, causing more than one tongue to wag when the twenty-two-year-old deputy sheriff took the seventeen-year-old to her senior prom. Remembering her mother's disapproval, Anne wondered if she should have stopped the attraction way back then, halting the small town suppositions.

But Joe had been the soul of discretion while they dated, caring for her, courting her. Seeing her through college, steadfast and strong. Coming to every race he could when free time was scarce for a new deputy. For a while she'd lived her dream as Joe's girl, then his wife. For those short years she'd had it all.

Noting her mother's look, she worked to push Joe out of mind. Maura inclined her head. "You saw him?"

"Yes."

Maura waited. Anne sat silent, stewing.

"And?"

"He hates me, resents me, wishes I'd never been born." Anne lifted her shoulders. "What would you expect?"

"He said that?" Her mother's tone heightened in indignation.

"No." Anne hesitated, remembering Joe's complete and utter silence. "No, he'd never say that, Mom. But the feelings were there. I read them in his face."

"Men are prideful creatures, Annie-Lou." Her mother slipped in the endearing name as though she used it every day. "They heal different from you and me."

"Or not at all."

"I don't believe that," rejoined her mother. "God gives us ample chance to move beyond. Choosing to forgive is ours alone. Same as choosing not to."

"I hurt him, Mom. Embarrassed him. Joe's always been a proud man."

"There's a reason pride is one of the seven deadly sins, girl," Maura reminded her. "They grow out of control with precious little encouragement."

"I know." Anne thought of the plans Joe laid before her when he proposed. The home he wanted to build. The family he longed for. She'd swept that out from under him by walking out. Slapping down his manhood. She'd spent a lot of time on that one, praying for forgiveness, an exoneration she knew was undeserved. His hardened countenance assured her no such thing was forthcoming. "Has he remarried?"

Her mother squawked. The click-clack of the needles intensified. "No. And I don't like you shouldering the blame for what went wrong between you," she spouted. She flashed a look of frustration Anne's way. "Anyone could see how unhappy you were, Anne. Desperate, even. I've no patience for a man who doesn't treat a woman right. If only you'd listened all them years before, when I warned you about dating him, a boy that much older. Didn't seem right, a boy his age, interested in a high school girl, and time proved me out."

"Mom, I—" Anne thought hard. This would be the perfect time to explain that Joe had nothing to do with her sudden departure. That *she* was the guilty one, not him. Never him.

But then her mother would want to know more. Was she ready to take responsibility? Field those questions and own her part? Anne bit back a sigh of cowardice. *No.*

"Does he have kids?" Based on Kyle's raging carnivore bellows from beyond the front door, she knew marriage wasn't requisite to procreation. Another stab of guilt hit.

Joe had shown her nothing but loving respect before their marriage. When the time had come, he'd loved her completely, quieting her fears of discovery with his caring. His gentleness. Joe McIntyre believed in doing the right thing always. Honor, first. He carried that trait into all aspects of his life.

"No." Maura shook her head, then smiled in Kyle's direction as a dinosaur met its demise in the spreading yew. "Goes out now and again. Dated somebody from Ogdensburg for a while. Jenna something or other. I heard she didn't take to his hunting and fishing habits."

Anne stood. Sitting was making her tired. Time to busy her hands. "He always loved tracking things through the woods. Working a stream. It was born in him. Look at the awards his father has won."

Jim McIntyre had claimed first prize in fishing and hunting derbies throughout the Northeast. As owner of a popular sportsmen's lodge, he'd made his life's passion his work. Joe came to his prowess naturally, growing up at his father's side. He'd been target shooting and fly-tying when most boys still tugged apron strings. That independence, his oneness with nature, had been part of the attraction. Of course his chiseled good looks hadn't hurt. Or the expanse of his chest, thick and broad. Pushing those thoughts aside, she busied her hands with dinner.

Keeping Joe in the past wouldn't be easy here, unlike Georgia. There, in the small town of Toccoa, she'd lived the life of a school teacher, raising her boy with tenderness and humor. She'd known acceptance, the warmth of a community that didn't delve into her history as long as she brought knowledge to their young. She'd sheltered herself in southern grace and hospitality, nestled in a cocoon of faith, hiding from the past.

Here, there would be daily reminders of what had been and what could have been. All she'd thrown away when fear took precedence. Here there was reckoning, something she'd put off a long time. She wasn't the same girl she'd been eight years before, the one who ran from the threat of discovery, then threw caution to the winds in a fit of temper. The passage of time had strengthened her.

Easy words. Thoughts of her behavior in Florida tweaked Anne's conscience. Loose. Immoral. She'd gone from one extreme to the other, trying to dislodge the guilt that laid claim to her soul. Guilt that festered for years.

She sighed, eyeing the boy as he raced a Hot Wheels Mustang across the porch, straight into the path of marauding velociraptors. She'd made more than one mistake in the time she'd been away. Kyle was living proof of her indiscretion. But she'd worked to re-center her soul after his birth, facing each day, one by one, until some small part of her felt good again. Whole.

"Forgiving and good," she quoted softly, her ears tuned to engine-like noises as a miniature 4X4 chased an errant T-Rex. "Abounding in love. To you, O Lord, I lift up my soul."

Easier said than done. Anne knew the drill. God was all loving, all forgiving. Ask and you shall receive, knock and the door will be opened. A quick learner, she could quote chapter and verse, but she was learned enough to realize the promises didn't add up in logical fashion.

Forgiveness and redemption, freely given, with no atonement? No penance or scourging, no righteous beating of her breast? That didn't make sense to a math teacher whose lessons dealt in absolutes. Anne gnawed her lower lip, unable to align belief with fact. That kind of inequity stuck in the craw of a scientific mind.

Tipping her chin up, she refused to dwell on the imbalance. She'd focus on the here and the now, give thanks for her blessings. Her boy, her health. The chance to help her mother. Much better to concentrate on what she had in her life. Not what she'd lost.

With Joe Michael McIntyre so close, that wouldn't be an easy task.

CHAPTER FOUR

Joe pulled into his driveway thinking this might have been the longest day in his life. Then, pondering the afternoon he'd walked into an empty apartment that used to hold a wife he loved, he changed his estimation.

Second-longest day.

She was still beautiful. Why did that make him angry? Did he want her ugly? Retribution for her sin?

"Okay, you." He envisioned a heavenly finger wagging Anne's way. "You broke a man's heart for no apparent reason. Ugliness for you, the rest of your days!"

Hadn't happened. Her willowy figure, perfect for a runner, had more curve than when they'd wed, but still bore an athletic grace.

And her hair. Walnut brown, set off by hazel eyes. They matched some days and contrasted others. He used to make a game out of picking different shirts for her, watching her eyes change color.

His chest ached at the thought of dredging everything up. The pain he felt to find her gone. He'd been afraid, knowing how depressed she seemed those last weeks.

Until he realized she'd just dumped him.

Now he wanted to strike back, even after all this time. The realization made him pause.

Hadn't he moved beyond this? He'd pushed their romance aside, just like she had, and gone on with his life.

He'd built their house. The cedar-sided A-frame overlooked the river, surrounded by trees and flowers on three sides. A beautiful yard thickened into a maple wood. The tall, gray trees dripped sap late winter, the liquid sweetness channeled in an intricate weave of tubes and gravity.

He could pray here. Think. Contemplate the wonders of nature, the beauty of the earth.

But his thoughts tonight centered on Annie, standing strong in his office. Facing him across the expanse of Route 11. Nodding politely as if he were any old boy.

He peeled off his uniform and jumped in the shower. Letting the warm water beat against the frustration, he worked to relax his tensed muscles. They'd constricted when he first laid eyes on her, and hadn't un-bunched yet.

The shower helped. That and a steak done over the fire, a potato roasted in its coals. No one to scold him about the dangers of cholesterol or the evils of carbs.

College buddies would visit sometimes. Fish. Hunt. They'd extol the beauty of his place, how their wives would never hear of being tucked away, off the main drag. It was malls and soccer clubs, all around.

He'd chosen differently, planning to raise his kids the way he was raised. Strong in faith, nurturing the creatures around them. Working for food rather than depending solely on a grocer's shelf.

He'd even set up a pigpen in the woods. Downwind, of course. Two porkers slated to be butchered and shared in the cold of November. Ribs for Thanksgiving? Naw, his mother wouldn't hear of that. Thanksgiving dinner was turkey, through and through. But those ribs would be a nice winter's barbecue.

The thought fell short. Somehow, celebrating his freedom had lost its sheen for the night.

Maybe for the year.

Forever?

He strode into the woods and harvested two dead trees for winter fuel. Using excess energy, he cut them into movable pieces, then carted them to his hydraulic wood-splitter.

He already had five face-cords ready. Double that should do fine. With the A-frame's open design and southern exposure, he was able to generate some solar heat most days. When frigid cold descended, he simply threw a few more logs on the fire, smiling at his non-existent heat bill.

It was a good life, all in all. Except when he was so lonely he could cry. Like tonight.

The mosquitoes drove him in at dusk. Their short months gave them robust appetites. Joe shook his head as he slid the screen door closed. He'd been chewed on enough today. He glanced at the TV and his Bible, both enjoying places of prominence in the great room. He huffed, weighing his options. Mindless entertainment or soul-searching scripture, geared to make him think and repent?

The TV won, hands down.

"Boog. How's it going?"

The forty-something craftsman looked up as Joe moved into the cutting area of Adirondack Woodcrafters. "Well enough. You drew Saturday duty, Chief?"

"I did." Joe ran a finger across the maple's smooth grain. "Beautiful work."

"Good design."

Boog wasn't big on taking credit. He exuded humble in a day when the word got little use. Boog Camden, a long-time member of the local business council and

Alcoholics Anonymous, was a rugged man with a gentleman's touch and a past he kept to himself. Joe sent him a steady look. "I think the craftsman sells himself short."

Boog shrugged, his countenance easy. "Thanks, Chief. Fresh coffee in the pot."

"I was hoping."

As Joe filled a mug, Boog continued, "I hear Maura's got herself some company. Your girl, I believe."

"Not mine, Boog. Not in a long time." Joe put a note of warning in his voice.

Boog nodded while he examined the curved front edge of the seat. "It needs to be just so," he explained as he eyed the curve, critical.

Joe shrugged. "A rocker's a rocker, isn't it?"

Boog looked up, surprised. "Mothers rock their babies in these. Feeding them. Consoling them. Can't have young mothers uncomfortable. Bad for production."

In over a decade of friendship, Boog had never brought up the topic of nursing mothers in casual conversation. Joe was pretty sure they had no reason to discuss it now, either. "Why would I need to know that?"

"Nothing comes to mind," Boog replied. Satisfied, he began sanding. "But you never know."

"I'm not keen on rumors, Boog. Your opinions on lactating women would better serve your female customers."

Boog nodded, affable. "I'll keep that in mind. Were you here about a chair?"

"Yes," Joe answered, peeved. He sipped his coffee, burnt his tongue and worked not to swear. He swiped a hand across his mouth, frustrated. "Not a rocker, either. Something hearty. A guy's chair." He set a picture of his chairs in front of Boog. "Like these, only with arms."

"A captain's chair." Boog nodded. "I can do it, sure. Won't be for a while, though. I've got some specials to finish up, and stock for the cybermall to have ready for Christmas orders."

That suited Joe. "No hurry. Just something I meant to do and didn't."

"Not like you," remarked Boog. "You're generally a season ahead."

"The seasons are sliding along," Joe admitted. He nodded to the seat-less rocker. "That's a fine piece, though. I like the press-back look. How much would that set someone back?"

"Three-eighty." Boog worked a tack rag across his fingers. "If you decide you want one, let me know. I'll cut you a deal. Though oak goes better in your front room," he added.

"I've no need for a rocker," Joe replied. "We ascertained that, right?"

"Needs change," Boog returned, patient. "Mark that, my friend. Needs change."

Annie was helping Maura up the church ramp when Joe pulled into Holy Trinity's lot on Sunday morning. They moved slowly, the ascent tedious. Anne offered easy escort, acting as if she had all the time in the world although bells pealed above.

A boy barreled back to them. Annie paused. Her mouth moved in reprimand. Quiet, the boy settled in, but his eyes darted as if he couldn't wait to run free. Peel off the constraining shirt. Chase a frog.

"Anne, is this your son?" An older church member stepped up to greet them as Joe approached the walk.

Joe heard the words, but couldn't believe them. *Her son?* Anne had a child? She nodded as they proceeded. At the door, she pivoted, glancing around.

Her eyes met his. Their gazes locked. He read discomfort in hers. Chagrined, she grimaced at the retreating backs of her mother and son, then moved his way. "She wouldn't go to Westside and there's only one service here. I'm sorry."

He stared, her words barely registering. "You have a son?"

Her face paled. She nodded. "Yes."

What he muttered wasn't pretty. His eyes went to her hands, noting the lack of jewelry. Not bothering to hide his derision, he stepped back. "Since he's too young to be mine, I'm going to assume you ran out on his father too."

He could have slapped her and caused less pain, but that was illegal, not to mention immoral. Men didn't hit women, not in his town, anyway.

But cut with words? No law against that.

Her chin wavered. She firmed it before she walked away, striding into the church as if she belonged there.

Grumbling, he turned as well, retracing his steps to his SUV.

It took effort not to gun the engine like a stupid teen. He eased down the road, in no mood to be placated, and walked into Westside Community, glowering.

A few whispered. Two older women nodded knowing heads. Most welcomed his unexpected arrival. Hands clasped his, men clapped him on the back, enjoining him to sit with them, share their spot with the Lord.

Through it all he envisioned Anne's face, the flash of pain his harshness inspired. Her reaction churned his stomach.

He spent the service praying for God to help him shut his big, fat mouth. Somehow, he'd have to invoke the "Thumper Rule" where Annie was concerned. If he couldn't say anything nice, he wouldn't say anything at all. That would prove hard, because there was so much he wanted to ask.

Starting with, "Why?"

CHAPTER 5

"Redmond's given me a one-year contract." Anne grinned as she hung up the phone. "Full benefits, junior high science program and a nice paycheck."

Maura's smile matched her daughter's. "Just what I prayed for. And Kyle?"

"I'm enrolling him as well," Anne affirmed.

"Redmond's a good school, Anne."

"It is." Anne nodded as a knot in her stomach untwisted. Her contract made it affordable for Kyle to attend Redmond; his tuition was gratis as long as Anne taught there. This would quiet talk of Forest Hills schools for her son. The topic just became a non-issue. She knew Maura wondered at her decision, her adamancy that Kyle attend the private school.

Explaining her choice was tricky. Her mother might be sick but she was sharp as a tack. Anne's touchiness about the past had caused the occasional raised brow, but no way could she launch into why Kyle would never set foot in Forest Hills schools without coming up with an acceptable explanation. An explanation her mother might see through.

Tell her.

The internal voice prodded her. *Wouldn't you want to know if something like that happened to Kyle?*

Anne shivered. Nothing like that would ever happen to Kyle. She'd see to it. She'd—

Uh huh. Lots of luck, girlfriend. Aren't you living proof of what parents don't know? Short answer, please.

Yes.

So do your best, make him strong, give him a solid base. Faith. Hope. Love. Cookies. Got it?

Anne faced off with the inner counselor of her conscience. *Like you know so much. You want to try it out here, facing the looks, the criticism, the constant appraisals?*

Her conscience offered a fake shudder. *Are ya' kiddin'? No way, no how. You go, girl. You're tough now. Give 'em what you got.*

Right. Piece of cake.

"Are you guys okay while I run?" Anne adjusted her waistband, trying to sort her thoughts.

Maura nodded, folding little pants and polos from the basket at her feet. "We're fine. If your run turns into a mini-marathon, don't fret. Kyle and I have things under control."

Anne smiled. She had a tendency to stroke out the miles once she began. Running the woods was sacred time. She could use some of that right now. "Thanks, Mom."

Kyle looked up from the porch. Legions of mixed-era dinosaurs intimidated one another as they trudged across aged gray decking. "Mind the slivers," Anne reminded him, frowning. The roughened surface could use a thorough sanding and some deck paint. She could ask Joe—

She paused, considered that option and discarded it quickly.

"I will," Kyle promised.

Anne swiped him a kiss. "See you in a bit. Which team's winning?"

"The ones with the biggest teeth." Kyle pumped a fist of victory. "Meat-eaters rule." A fierce looking T-

Rex took down an unsuspecting veggie-saurus, uttering a roar of triumph.

"Couldn't they have a tea party? Sit around a campfire? Sing *Kumbaya*?"

"Girl stuff," pronounced her son. "Mom, you're standing in the Great Lagoon."

"Oh. Sorry." Laughing, she headed down the drive. "Be good for Grammy."

He waved, immersed in a battle over dwindling tree stars. Anne rolled her eyes, thinking they ought to expound on peaceful mediation. Conflict resolution.

Or just celebrate the fact that her son was a boy. As long as he kept his aggression to dino play, she saw no harm. Unlike the hostility she felt in the village. Different story there.

She'd wanted a hair trim the week before. Charity Boyd shut the door in her face. Anne had backed away slowly, not allowing the stylist the gratification of tears. She'd cried those later. Much later.

Leila Freeman had sent Anne a sympathetic look through the window, then called, offering to trim Anne's hair at home. As an employee, it was hard to stand up to your boss, she explained, her voice hesitant.

Anne refused her offer. Her stubborn streak reared its head, and she rejected one of the few altruistic gestures she'd received. Then the butcher refused to bone out the roast she'd wanted. No explanation, no apologies. Just a flat 'no', his eyebrow arched in challenge.

She wasn't oblivious to the looks that accompanied her throughout town. That made the decision to shop elsewhere easy.

She'd been part of Forest Hills for over twenty years. A part of her longed for the acceptance she'd known. But reality smacked her upside the head. Anne Kellwyn was persona non grata now, with little recourse.

Her pride took the slap down. She glanced at her watch, wondering how long it would take to work off the hurt bestowed by a town that saw her as a betrayer.

Was Joe behind the shunning? Her heart said no, but her head remembered his expression outside the church.

Did he hate her that much?

Better question: why shouldn't he?

Even better question: would he have hated her if she'd confessed eight years before, told him the truth? Gotten it off her chest?

Moot point now. She'd been afraid then. Not of Joe's actions. God hadn't made a gentler man.

But his reactions? The hurt? The disappointment that was sure to follow? The embarrassment of knowing your wife slept with her running coach at age thirteen?

No way could she face that. And the pictures Tom had, making it look like she tempted him, drew him... No, there was no way Anne could deal with the world seeing those. Not then. Not now.

Instead she'd left, gone to Florida, enrolled in school to get her Master's degree. And partied like a maniac trying to numb the pain of leaving Joe.

How stupid. For over a year she became the kind of woman Tom Baldwin accused her of being. She shook her head at the senselessness.

But she had Kyle. From evil, came good, and she didn't want the boy to see his mother ostracized. Banished.

Would Kyle ever see the goodness in Forest Hills, the way they celebrated the success of their young? Not unless they stayed a long while. Redmond had contracted her for a year.

After that, their choices depended on Maura's situation. With Anne's help, maybe they could buy time. Regain some of her mother's lost strength.

Toccoa would welcome her back at any time. They'd said as much. There she'd become a well-respected teacher and coach.

Adjusting her sweatband, she ran on, pushing through the initial tightness as her calf muscles offered protest.

At least at church there'd been no further altercations since the initial one with Joe. Pastor Wilson welcomed her as though she'd never left, and his example paved the way. Sure, there was talk. But nothing malicious came up at Holy Trinity and she was grateful for the respite. Now, if only the rest of the town could follow suit...

"Anne! Nice to see you. Have a good run."

Flashing a smile, Anne returned Sally's wave and gave a quick glance to her watch. The abbreviated time deepened her grin. She always ran faster when she was upset. Five-forty miles on a training run. Pretty quick.

The county festival was coming up. Area businesses sponsored a road race with a nice chunk of prize money. Anne was tempted to enter, vying for the win. Not because of the money, but how ironic would it be to accept that first-prize envelope from the very people who refused to do business with her?

But that would mean facing them. Standing on the grandstand in front of festival crowds. She wasn't that gutsy. She could handle rejection one on one, but facing an unfriendly crowd of hundreds? Thousands?

No.

Scripture told how Christ met a similar reception in his hometown. People scoffed at his teachings, treating him with disdain. They laughed, wondering how he got so full of himself. Teacher, indeed. Rabbi. He was just plain old Jesus, a little too big for his britches in the locals' estimation. They shunned his word and negated his miracles.

But he toughed it out, big time, right through the end.

The big difference? Jesus didn't deserve the town's enmity. Anne had earned it.

"Lend me your strength, Lord," she prayed, rounding the four-mile mark. "Let me smile in the face of my enemies."

While smiling might be a little optimistic, she'd come back for one simple reason. Her mother needed her.

Soon she'd be teaching, her days filled with students, her nights devoted to her mother's well-being and first grade homework. There'd be little time for wayward thought and guilty introspection.

She hoped.

CHAPTER SIX

Annie took a job at Redmond. Tom Baldwin pondered this new circumstance as he studied his current women's team during a training run.

Maura's weakening condition must have drawn Annie home. That was the word on the street. Probably accurate, too. She wouldn't have returned, otherwise, right? Unless—

Thoughts torn, Tom contemplated this new wrinkle. Annie had been a once-in-a-lifetime kind of girl. He didn't know that then. He hadn't realized how hard she'd be to replace. A rookie mistake, one he'd regretted for too many years.

He skirted a tree root, thinking hard. He'd been unable to recreate the wonder of that time with Annie. Her innocence. Her unabashed love. Hero worship, big time, longing for someone to take care of her.

He'd tried, often enough, but nothing took her place. Not then. Maybe now—

Now that she'd returned—

He might have the chance he'd craved for years.

Straight ahead, his newest protégé set the pace for her older teammates. Tom's gut twisted as Missy Volmer moved, French-braids slapping her slim shoulders with each step. She'd lost her mother to cancer last spring and her father had voiced reservations about letting a youngster run with juniors and seniors. Briggs Volmer made Tom promise to take good care of her, because Briggs' time was swallowed by work and Missy's younger brothers.

Tom studied Missy's style. Petite. Sassy. Competitive, even at this young age. And longing for love, for someone to spend time with her. Make her feel special.

Oh, yeah. He'd take care of her.

Moving to the outside, Tom passed the main pack of runners and fell into step beside the eighth-grader. She glanced up and answered his smile with one of her own.

Tom matched her pace, then shifted, pushing her to keep up. She grinned at his tactic and matched him, step for step.

He nodded approval with a quick wink and watched her smile deepen.

Yeah, he'd look after Missy. A talented runner, she could go places, given the right training. Her aggressive style might be just enough to edge Annie's records.

His heart quickened, but he calmed things down swiftly. No sense jumping to conclusions. Time would tell. In the meantime, if Missy's father didn't have the sense to spend quality time with the girl, Tom would fill the void.

"We don't need her kind, no sir," remarked a deep female voice.

Joe listened from one grocery aisle over, unabashed.

"Head out of town after everyone and their brother supported her, turning her back on a good coach like Tom, then dumping the nicest guy in the world. I closed the door in her face," Charity continued.

"I wish I could have," another voice confessed. "My boss said old feuds are best forgotten and anyone with a clink of change in their pocket is welcome at his counter."

"That's the beauty of havin' your own business," professed the beauty shop proprietor. "I say who stays. If she wants to drop the old woman off, that's one thing, but I ain't serving her, no way, no how. And who does she think she is, showing up after all this time with a kid? No," Charity Boyd's hard voice mocked her given name, "I don't need the likes of Annie Kellwyn in my waiting room, chasing other folk away. Times are hard enough."

The words gnawed Joe's belly. They weren't the first derogatory comments he'd heard regarding Anne. Rafe Conti, a hunting partner who ran the local meat market, seemed proud to announce he'd refused to cut a special roast for her Sunday dinner.

Joe considered the situation as he walked the beat. Other than himself, no one in town had a beef with Anne, except maybe Tom Baldwin. Tom had developed her talent, investing countless hours in her training. Selecting the best races, Tom made Annie the darling of the Northeast running circuit. Tom fashioned the gangly girl into a first-class contender. Oh, Annie put the time in. She'd trained with a winner's spirit, her eye on the promise of a scholarship. Tom stuck by her through thick and thin. He'd even been a pall bearer at her father's funeral.

But other than Tom and Joe's family, Anne's departure hadn't hurt a soul. Why were the locals ostracizing her?

Because of him.

Joe growled. She'd hurt him, so they'd hurt her. Of all the contrary notions. He swiped a hand across the nape of his neck, annoyed, then tipped his cap to the Pritchard sisters, the harmonic thunk of aluminum walkers announcing their approach. The aging women beamed and Joe paused his walk. "Miss Mary? Miss Martha?" He nodded to the elderly spinsters in turn. "Nice day."

Mary's eyes lit as she grasped his hand, her chin angled homeward. "Our mums are quite lovely this year, don't you think, Joe? Just now coming into their own."

Joe cocked a brow of interest. "I noticed that right off, Miss Mary. I'm especially fond of the new ones." His look of appreciation swept the noble front yard. "Pink and white."

She squeezed his forearm. "Mauve-dappled-ivory."

He grinned. "Always the teacher."

"They *are* new, Joe." Her tone said she was happy he noticed. "Come spring, I'll give you a slip for your place. They like full sun, but a little shade won't hurt."

Joe nodded, appreciative. "I've got just the spot. Don't you forget, now."

"Oh, she won't, Chief. Her memory's sharp. Matches her tongue." A slight thump of Martha's walker punctuated the assertion.

Mary reared back. "Why, Martha—"

"Don't 'why, Martha' me," retorted the older sister. "Facts are facts. Weren't you just saying you couldn't understand the likes of that girl, running off on a fine man like our Chief?" Martha turned back to Joe, her expression pointed. "*I* said it's none of our concern. A married couple needs to work things out for themselves and people should stop running her down." She glared at her younger sister, her chin firm.

Joe couldn't disagree. "You're right, of course."

"Like she knows anything about marriage," spouted Mary, her chinks pink. She pressed Joe's arm again. "Three dates in eighty years. Whew hoo." Releasing her grip, she fanned herself in mock amazement. "A wealth of experience."

"Enough to know right from wrong." Martha's jaw tightened as she compressed her lips, eyes tight.

Uh, oh.

Joe saw no easy way out. Once the old girls got going, they could carry on forever. He glanced at his watch and tipped his cap. "Ladies. Always a pleasure. Enjoy your walk."

That paused them momentarily. "You have a spot turned for those mums come spring, Joe."

"I'll do that, Miss Mary." He turned and nodded to Martha. "I appreciate your kindness, Miss Martha. All around."

She looked him in the eye, her expression frank. "A body doesn't always get a second chance to set things right, Chief. I expect a smart man like you knows that."

Wise words. Joe met her frank gaze and nodded. "I'll keep it in mind."

Mary's sharp words had hit home. Like so many, she pointed a finger at Anne, excusing Joe.

Joe worked his jaw, pensive. A town defending their police chief against a girl. If he weren't so ashamed, the thing would be downright amusing.

He hadn't seen Annie in weeks. With the college influx, he'd been busy. Clarkson was hosting a soccer game on Saturday, and St. Lawrence a cross-country invitational. Luckily the two SUNY schools were enjoying a quiet opening weekend.

The invasion of traffic kept their small force busy. Once the coming weekend ended, life would return to a semblance of normal. Sure, the college crowds were back. That was expected. But the parents would head back home, outside of St. Lawrence County.

The exodus would give him a chance to think. Breathe. Contemplate how he'd handled things so far.

Mucked up, totally.

To avoid controversy, he kept going to Westside, thinking prayer was prayer. Great concept for a naïve guy. The reality? Not even close. Westside's young pastor breathed fire and brimstone like a cartoon dragon, until Joe was fairly sure he had no hope of salvation.

Disheartening news for a guy dealing with anger issues.

But his absence at Holy Trinity gave Anne and her mother leeway with Pastor Wilson, the gentle man who'd shepherded their church for nearly two decades.

Joe made it a point not to watch for Annie's car, a gray Civic, Georgia plate 2935 YMN. He hadn't set out to memorize the tag, but the fact that it named their ages made for an easy mark. She was twenty-nine on June tenth. He'd be thirty-five come January.

But if the pulse of the town ran as he suspected, Anne endured a rough month. Even the part of him that wanted her punished took no pleasure in that.

Not much, anyway.

A Saturday night pennant race baseball game was half-over on ESPN when his phone rang. He reached out a tired hand, almost hoping for a telemarketer. Glancing at the late hour, he figured most self-respecting salesmen had gone to bed. He yawned, then grabbed the phone. "Chief McIntyre."

"We've got some trouble here with your ex," reported Kim Riccitti. "Best get back."

Aw, Annie, what have you done? His was a silent protest, with no one to hear or care. Pulling into the municipal lot minutes later, Joe scanned for her car.

Not there.

Glancing down the road, he scowled. No sign of the Civic. Wondering, he strode into the station.

"Jenna?" Spotting the woman half-slouched in a chair, he hoped he didn't look as confused as he felt. He eyed Kim. "What's going on?"

"DWI. Rick pulled her over, tested for levels, then confiscated the keys. She's here overnight. We couldn't find anyone to take her home."

"Jenna." Bending, Joe gave his former girlfriend a questioning look. A part of him was glad Annie hadn't broken the law, but the less magnanimous side would have taken distinct pleasure in locking his ex-wife away. An eight-year stint in solitary ought to do it. Grimacing, he shut the feeling down, concentrating on the situation at hand.

Jenna Reichter. They'd dated off and on, but the relationship never went to flash stage. Still, she was a nice girl who didn't generally tie one on while driving an aggravating two-lane road on one of the busiest weekends of the year. He pulled up a chair. "What's going on?"

"I'm drunk," she wailed, spewing breath that had him sliding his chair back.

Okay, now that the obvious was out of the way... Joe drew a breath, his appreciation for fresh air rising. "I see that. Why?"

"Because I had too much beer."

Joe counted to ten. "I know *how* you got that way. Why did you get drunk? This is a serious charge, Jenna."

She nodded, eyes streaming, as if she understood the gravity of a DWI.

Wrong again.

"Because Todd broke up with me when he started dating Emily, who used to be my best friend until she two-timed me by dating my boyfriend who still has my CD collection, including the newest one from Lady Antebellum." She blotted her eyes, smearing her mascara. "I want it back."

"The CD collection?"

"Nooooooo!" she wailed again. "Todd. He can keep the CD collection if he dumps her and takes me. I don't know what to do without him, Joe." She wailed into the tissues again. Joe sighed. Kim sent him an amused look he didn't dare return.

He slid the lined garbage can Jenna's way. "Listen, I'm no expert, but why do you want a guy who doesn't love you? Who doesn't want you and only you?" He leaned forward. "You're a great girl. Pretty. Usually smart." He tried to look compassionate while avoiding direct breath confrontation. It wasn't easy. "There are lots of prospects out there. One of them will be the knight in shining armor you're looking for. Stop trying to hurry the process. Let things unfold as they should."

"Oh, Joe," she crowed, the beer raising her pitch. He leaned back in self-defense. "You're so smart. I'm glad you're my friend."

"Well, your friend has to lock you up," he replied. "We'll release you in the morning. Right now, you need to catch some sleep. Kim has evening watch. Mike's on overnight. Rick's doing the Sunday twelve-hour shift. Any questions?"

She nodded, raising tragic eyes to his. "Where's the bathroom? I'm going to hurl."

He got her there in time, then turned, giving Kim a thumbs-up. "All yours, Officer."

She shook her head, listening to the sounds of beer-induced human misery in the ladies' room. "Thanks, Chief."

Joe bit back words of self-recrimination as he pulled into the Kellwyn's driveway on Sunday afternoon.

The place needed work. When was the last time he'd sent his brother over? Two years back?

Nearly three, he realized, feeling the guilt rise. Since he was here, he might as well look the place over.

A dog barked down the road, but all was quiet at the bungalow nestled along the western edge of the woodland. More than a little self-conscious, he moved up the steps, then tapped on the door.

No answer.

Of course not. He hadn't been on the same page with this girl in a long time. Maybe never. He knocked again.

This time he heard footsteps. Annie appeared, wearing loose sweats and a t-shirt, a sweatband snug around her forehead. She stared at him, mouth open, before catching herself. "What do you want?"

Well, he hadn't expected warmth. He nodded to the small porch. "Can we talk a minute? Please?"

She stepped out the door. Eyeing him, she moved to the stoop, arms clenched around her middle. She sat, her back stiff. He followed suit. "I brought you something."

Great opening. About as lame as he could get, as if offering a gratuitous token could make up for the town's foolishness when he'd been the worst of all, letting them shun her without stepping in. His mother would blush to think he had it in him. Leaning over, he set the oblong package in Anne's lap.

"You brought me meat?" She shook her head in disbelief. "A good hunting season?" Her voice smacked of sarcasm, her eyes shooting sparks of not-so-happy-to-see-you fire.

"I got the meat from the butcher shop," Joe explained. "Rafe sends his apologies. Promises it will never happen again."

"Right." Her tone didn't sound forgiving. He put a hand out, indicating she should take it. She gave him a look of frank dismissal and refused, silent.

Joe rose, restless, and started to pace. "People got protective once you left. You know how it is here, Annie. Clannish. They look after their own."

"Do they?" She raised her gaze. "I was one of their own. I don't see too many remembering that."

"You left," he reminded her. "You shook Forest Hills's dust from your high-tech running shoes and took off. People don't forgive easy. It takes time."

"Eight years should have been more than enough," she retorted, setting the roast down with a thump. "Especially for something that wasn't their business in the first place."

Her words stopped his movements. He stared at her, thoughts racing, then bent closer. "It was my business, and I don't have a clue what went wrong between us." There she was, one on one, with no one but him to hear her response. Moving closer, he pressed on. "Why'd you leave me, Anne?"

Her throat muscles clenched. Her eyes filled. The urge to hold her swept him. He fought it down as being so far beyond stupid as to be immeasurable. "Tell me. Please."

Her shoulders shuddered with restrained tears, but she shook her head, stoic, staring beyond him. "I wasn't who you thought I was. That's all I could see. You thought you'd won some kind of grand prize when the reality was quite the opposite. If I'd been half the person you deserved, I could have stayed. But I had no right to be there, be your wife."

Her words made no sense. "You're talking in riddles. You had every right. You were my wife, my lover. My first in everything. I didn't have a plan that didn't include you, Annie. Our family. Our home. Then you were gone, without a word, and I didn't know what to think." There. He'd said his piece. He was careful not to add how he'd used his connections to trace her path, eventually finding her name in the registry of Master's candidates at Florida State.

The shock he felt then swept back. She'd left him high and dry and returned to school? The discovery had pushed his anger. Watching her face now, he didn't think he'd win points by admitting he'd tracked her down like a hunted criminal.

She stared at nothing, looking tired. "My leaving had nothing to do with you, Joe. It was all me. I'm the one who messed up."

One tear spilled over, tracking down her cheek. He resisted the urge to brush it away, more than a little mad he felt the urge at all.

Anne drew a deep breath, then exhaled long and slow. The slow air helped. Her tears paused. "I hated myself then. It took a lot of years to move beyond that.

To start a new life. I didn't intend to come back here, put you through this, but my choices were limited. Mom wants to die at home."

"It's that serious?" He tried to meet her eye, but she averted her face.

"She could go any time. She's got late stage cardiomyopathy on top of her diabetes; her heart can't beat strongly enough to pump the blood through her body and with her weight, the diabetes has cycled out of control. Medicine kept things in check for a while, but now, without a transplant..." She trained her gaze on the trees. "An infection, a cold, a virus that causes vomiting in you and me...Any of those could be her death knell. Her other health problems have kept her off the transplant list and the available medications are no longer effective. It's a matter of time."

"Anne."

Still she didn't look at him.

"I'm sorry. I didn't realize how serious her condition was."

"Because you don't come by."

No argument there. She continued, "You think I can't tell that things are falling apart around here? Loose railings, slivered wood. Leaky faucets and mildew-damaged ceilings. Carpets musty from a rainy spring. Joe, she's an old woman. She never did you harm."

Not exactly true. Maura made no secret of not liking him, convinced he was too old and too ordinary for her Olympic-contender daughter.

When Anne pushed aside dreams of going to a nationally ranked Division One university, Maura and Tom blamed him. Neither one acknowledged that Anne had a rare focus for such a young woman. But Joe saw Annie's strength, her inner goals. With her father gone, staying at a well-respected local university with a great running program made perfect sense.

And kept her close enough to date, then court. He saw no problem in that, whatsoever. From his perspective, she'd made a good choice.

Maura and Tom didn't see things that way. They saw opportunities missed. They thought he'd wrangled her to stay close for his own selfish purposes.

He hadn't, even though he longed to do just that. Annie had come to the conclusion on her own.

He thought of the anger in Maura's eyes when he'd confronted her after Anne's disappearance, wanting to know where his wife had gone. She'd folded those thick arms across her middle, clamped her lips and hadn't breathed a word. Just looked at him as though he was pond scum, well rotted.

Joe drew a deep breath. Maura's distaste then didn't allow him latitude to let things slide like he had now. There was no excuse for the condition of the house. He bore the brunt of the criticism and nodded. "I'll make it right."

Anne glanced his way. "That would be good."

"You working tomorrow?"

She nodded, but didn't offer where. That was okay. He'd already heard about the job at Redmond. Not much got missed on the Forest Hills grapevine. He glanced around. "I've got the day off. I'll be by first thing, get things started."

"All right." She handed him the package of meat. "Take this. You shouldn't bring me things."

He hoped his expression registered how silly she sounded. "It's a hunk of meat. Cut the way you requested last week. I think as long as we make a rule to keep all gifts protein-related, we're okay."

She let out a long breath. "You heard."

"Too much," he retorted. "Listen, I'm sorry for the way you've been treated. I only just got wind of the seriousness, but I'll put a stop to it. It's hard enough coming back with all our history. There's no call for the town to make things more difficult than they already are."

"They love you, Joe."

He shrugged, staring into the deepening shade. "Yeah. Well."

She stood and brushed off the seat of her pants. He wasn't surprised to find he still thought her cute in sweats. So much of their romance had been played out at cross-country meets and track invitationals, that seeing her in standard gray sweats seemed normal.

But eight years of abnormal had intervened and the love of the century lasted six short months.

He wouldn't press more today, though. She seemed done in. He'd piece things together later, plug some holes. If he lowered the pistols, she might tell him why she made the choices she did. What made her so desperately unhappy in a marriage that brought him nothing but bliss until she fell apart.

The little boy charged through the door right then. "Mom! I did it. Just when the mouse thought it was safe, I...," stealthy pause, "set...," another one, longer this time, his Anne-eyes wide, "my...," this pause was accompanied by a triumphant clamp down of the cardboard lid and a gap-toothed grin, "trap." Holding up the box, the boy grinned crafty success.

"Awesome," Joe noted, smiling because he couldn't help himself. "You gonna let him go?"

"Or keep him as a pet," the boy suggested, looking at his mother, expectant.

"After being free all his life, how do you think he'd feel, penned in glass, scraping walls he can't see?" Anne's voice held the wisdom of motherhood, her look thoughtful.

Kyle sighed. "Yes, Ma'am." Eyeing the small rodent, he said, "Come on, little fella. I'm going to find you the very best and most wonderful place to live." After long moments of study, the boy picked out a copse of pine and liberated the mouse. Bent low, he laughed as the rodent scurried in two different directions before choosing a third, heading back toward the house.

Anne groaned.

Joe grimaced.

Kyle laughed in delight. "Maybe I can catch him again tomorrow," he caroled.

Joe cleared his throat to fight off a laugh. "We'll put the mice at the top of the list," he promised, pushing away from the step.

Anne sent a bemused look her son's way, then turned back to Joe, shaking her head. "I'd be grateful."

He headed back to his truck. "Let your mom know I'll be around, okay? I don't want to scare her."

Anne moved toward the door, roast in hand. "I will." She hoisted the roast slightly. "Thank you."

He didn't try to sort out the feelings that swept him. Too much, too soon. He just knew it felt good to see a hint of her smile. A smile he'd fallen in love with over a decade ago, and one he hadn't been privy to in a long while.

"You're welcome."

CHAPTER 7

"Anne."

A male voice hailed her as Anne hurried down the junior high hall. She smiled at a clutch of girls before she turned, gratified by their answering grins. She'd wondered about the adjustment to younger teens when she'd been offered this position; in Georgia she'd taught upperclassmen, writing college letters of recommendation for earnest juniors and seniors.

Week three, and she loved her job. She taught physical science overall, and earth science to those who forged ahead of the mainstream.

I'm having a ball, she thought, dodging a crew of middle school soccer players as she located the source of the voice. "Bruce. Hi."

Bruce Kingston stepped up to her, shaking his head, smiling broadly. "You even walk fast," he grumbled, making a face. "Listen, St. Lawrence has another invitational this weekend."

She nodded. She'd seen the newspaper notice. The university was hosting a large-scale cross-country event.

He inclined his head. "Like to go?"

She stared. "You mean, like a—"

"Date," he filled in, grinning. "That's exactly what I mean. We could get lunch or take a picnic, see the races." He lifted his shoulders lightly. "The weather's supposed to be nice and we won't be saying that much longer."

True. Still...

Anne shook her head. "I'm sorry, Bruce, I've got too much going on. Weekends are my time with Mom. She's so tired at night that she nods off after dinner. Saturdays and Sundays are the only time we have when she's awake. Talkative."

He frowned. "I'm sorry. I didn't realize." Studying a curving crack in the floor, he re-strategized. "If I nabbed a wheelchair, do you think your mother would enjoy going? As long as the weather holds?"

"We've got a wheelchair," she admitted, thinking. "And she was just saying how she missed going to the races. Watching the runners." She smiled, picturing her mother on the sidelines as she'd been long ago. "I'll ask her, Bruce." She started to turn, then swung back. "Uh, Bruce..."

He looked at her, his expression easy. "Spit it out, Anne. It can't be that bad."

"My son would be with us."

To his credit, he simply nodded. "Kyle, right?"

She sharpened her eyes. "How did you know that?"

He smiled. "When you're going to ask a pretty lady out, it pays to do your homework. Prepare to battle any dragons she may sling your way."

"Bruce Kingston, dragon slayer and math teacher, extraordinaire."

He laughed. "That's me." His gaze rose. Sharpened. "We have company."

Anne turned. Except for after-school events, all the kids had left nearly forty-five minutes before. That made Joe's footsteps louder. More foreboding. If the look on his face was any indication, they had trouble. He headed straight for them, frowning. "Anne, your mom's not well. I came to get you."

Panic seized her. She couldn't find her voice. *Not now, God,* she prayed silently, fighting the buzz in her system. *Not yet. I just got here. I'm not ready to say goodbye.*

Bruce stepped forward. "Shall I take you home?"

The hand Joe placed under her arm was almost gentle enough to offset the steel in his tone. "I've got her." He started to turn, then eyed her stack of books. "You need anything else? Jacket? Purse?"

"Yes." Handing him the books, she hurried down an adjacent corridor. Within seconds she returned, her purse and jacket slung over one arm. "Let's go. Good night, Bruce."

"I'll see you tomorrow, Anne."

Joe gave a slight nod to the other man. Using a long stride to keep up with her hurried one, he butted the door open with his hip, holding it ajar. Only then did she realize he still had her books. "Oh, I'm sorry," she exclaimed, holding out her hands. "I can take those."

Joe met her look of concern with equanimity. "I've got 'em."

Arriving at the cruiser he opened her door, handed her the pile of books once she was settled, then moved to his side.

The trip home took twenty minutes if traffic was light. Anne sucked a deep breath, staring out the window, clasping one hand in the other to keep from fidgeting. A twenty-minute ride trapped in a car with the man whose heart she'd broken years ago.

Talk about awkward.

"Did you call the doctor?" she asked, deciding her mother was a safe topic.

He shook his head, working his inner right cheek with his tongue. He did that when worried. "She wouldn't let me. She assured me she wasn't at death's door, and that you had an after school meeting so you'd be late, but..." He paused. His jaw tightened. "She didn't look good so I came for you." He went silent then, eyes straight ahead. The whir of tires against blacktop made the only sound for long, uncomfortable minutes. "How'd the meeting go?"

"Huh?" She looked at him, puzzled, then shrugged. "Oh. Fine. It was inter-department, math and science. That's why Bruce was there."

His gaze sharpened.

"We planned strategies to augment one subject with the other to better prepare the kids for the Regents expectations. Graphing, probabilities, tying scientific principle with mathematic logic." She almost groaned, wondering why she was discussing scientific principle with Joe McIntyre, her former husband. A man who still had the power to make her draw a deep breath by proximity alone.

"You like teaching?"

Another safe subject. Anne nodded. "Love it. I get to talk about my favorite subjects, science and math. I showed them how inter-related learning is by reading a Ray Bradbury short story today, linking science to everyday life. Or science fiction."

"You're good at your job." It was an observation, not a compliment.

"Yes."

"But then, you were good at everything you put your hand to," he added, his voice thoughtful.

Clutching her books, she sensed his train of thought. *Except our marriage.* But this was not the time to delve. She wasn't sure it would ever be the time. Not when the past locked her in knots. Joe pulled into the drive and shut off the engine.

He followed her to the house. She waved him off, protesting, "Joe, it's probably just one of her spells. She's good at recognizing them. I appreciate you coming for me, but we'll be fine."

He didn't growl, didn't glare. Just gave her a steadfast look inherent to peace officers and nodded to the door. "I'm staying."

Maura lay in bed, her breathing level. Drawing up the covers from the footboard, Anne checked her legs. "The swelling is worse," she whispered. "Her heart can't circulate blood properly. Fluid builds up." Sliding a thick pillow under her mother's calves, she fumbled as the covers tangled.

"Here." Gentle, Joe slid an arm under Maura's legs, lifting them. Annie applied the pillow, then nodded. Careful, he lowered her onto the plumped softness.

Moving to the kitchen, Anne counted pills in a bottle. "There are two more than there should be," she said, worried.

"Diuretics?"

"Yes. They dry her mouth and she hates that. Says it makes her feel like an old lady."

Joe eyes widened, but he made no comment.

Anne grimaced. "I know. She *is* an old lady. She just doesn't want to feel like one."

The rumble of a bus drew their attention. Short seconds later, Kyle dashed through the door. He flung his book bag one way, his jacket another. "I've got homework," he announced, then stared up at Joe. "Do you know about dinosaurs?" he asked, his face wondering.

Joe nodded. Stooped low. "St. Lawrence County's reigning dinosaur expert, at your service. What do you need to know?"

Kyle's face brightened. "Everything," he declared, reaching for a cookie from the jar on the counter. "Can I have two?"

"May I?"

"May I have two?"

"Yes." Anne took a pill and a glass of water into her mother's bedroom. When she returned, she saw Kyle curled next to Joe on the sofa, studying a book on prehistoric eras.

The naturalness of the scene played out like a dream come true. A sense of déjà vu enveloped her, remembering a maturing girl's thoughts of home and family with the man before her. The thought of love and laughter, holidays and children, swept in. What could have been, if only she'd been a whole lot smarter.

Joe's cell phone rang. He answered it offhand, still studying creatures. As the call progressed, he unwound himself from the couch and stood. For just a moment, his hand palmed the boy's ruff of curls. "All right, Jenna. I'm glad you're better, too." He glanced at his watch. "I'll be by directly."

Jenna. Anne choked back the glimmer of hope. Jenna was the girl her mother mentioned. The one who didn't take to Joe's hunting and fishing habits. Everyone knew if you fell in love with a North Country man, hunting and fishing were part of the package. That's how it was.

Not like she cared. She straightened as he grabbed his faded Notre Dame baseball cap. He tapped the boy on the head. "See you, Bud."

"Yeah, thanks," muttered Kyle, entrenched. "I'll remember that stuff about velociraptors. They sound really cool."

"He's not six years old, yet." Glancing toward Kyle, Anne voiced concern as she walked Joe out. "You're teaching him about velociraptors?"

"By theory of analogical relationship." Joe grinned at her confusion, his eyes crinkling. He leaned in, the smell of rugged man and aftershave teasing her senses. "I likened raptors to women." Before she could protest, he continued, "Travel in packs, voracious hunters, small minded." His grin widened as he pulled the brim of his cap down.

"That's not funny." Except it was.

"It is if you're a guy," he replied. "I've got to work tomorrow. I'll head back once I'm done. Keep going."

"That should be fine."

He glanced around, awkward. "I'm sorry for letting things go like this." He mulled a stone by his feet for long seconds. "It wasn't right."

"No." She stared at the same stone, then shrugged. "But coming here wouldn't have been easy. I know my mother hasn't been friendly to you." The guilt associated with that struck deep. Maura's negative feelings about Joe faded as Anne matured, then married him.

They roared back when Maura suspected Joe of abusing Anne, jumping to that conclusion as a combination of Anne's actions and silence.

She'd let her mother assume the worst about a good man, rather than face her shame. Another sin, another chain of lies. Would it ever end?

"A man can't always choose between what's easy and what's not," he answered softly. "I should have taken better care of things."

"You're doing it now." Anne glanced at her watch. "Aren't you supposed to be somewhere?"

"Yes." He strode to his car, then paused. Turned back. "I'll be by to take you to work in the morning."

His words brought realization. "I forgot my car."

He smiled. "Doors are locked?"

She nodded.

"It'll be fine. What time do you have to be there?"

"Six-forty-five."

"I'll be here at six-twenty. Your mom will be okay with the boy?"

"Morning's her good time."

"And there's nothing you need a car for tonight?" At the shake of her head, Joe nodded. "I'll see you in the morning, then." He tipped his cap as he left.

She inclined her head, her hand on the porch rail. A rail that now stood solid beneath her fingers. Her lips curved as she tugged. No give, whatsoever. Solid and tight.

Like the man who fixed it, she mused. Kyle's voice hailed her. Laughing, she went in and shooed him out. "Go play," she ordered. "Winter comes early and lasts forever. Soak up some vitamin D and fresh air."

"Where do I get them?"

She smiled as she busied her hands in the kitchen. "Vitamin D comes from the sun. Fresh air from God. Go enjoy both."

He grabbed her in a big hug. "I love you, Mom."

Her throat thickened. No matter what else happened, Kyle was a blessing. A gift from God to jump-start her on a path of righteousness. She pushed down the urge to get mushy. "Go on. Get out of here, or I'll cover you with kisses." She made a monstrous swoop for him, missing deliberately. He laughed and ran outside, screeching his escape.

Anne's eyes strayed to where Joe and Kyle had shared guy talk moments before.

Did he wonder about Kyle? He hadn't asked, and she wasn't sure what to tell him if he did. That she was young and stupid, grasping at anything to make her feel whole again? Fill a void? Take his place?

Joe wouldn't understand that. The concept of choosing sin wouldn't occur to him. For her, the partying and men were a buffer, a way to forget.

Except she didn't.

Her years in Toccoa had given her courage, but Anne was no one's fool any more. Uh, uh. She'd known no reckoning, no atonement. Surely God required some form of reparation. Something tangible.

She'd gone from a frightened adolescent to a self-destructive young adult, trying to chase the pain, but shadows lingered, ever ready, skirting her consciousness.

Time and faith had lent their strength. What happened to a thirteen-year-old girl was part of a past best left buried. With that thought, she moved to start supper, and almost fooled herself into believing it was possible.

CHAPTER 8

Saturday dawned bright. Tom Baldwin slid a grin and a wink to Missy Volmer. The eighth grader blushed, then winked back, sending a clear signal.

Oh, yes.

Tom nodded his encouragement. All this girl needed was someone to invest in her. If Missy's father couldn't be bothered, Tom would see to the task. With her distraught family dynamics, Missy was the kind of girl that flourished under a little extra male attention.

Meeting her gaze, he raised a brow of approval before turning away.

He liked knowing he still had it. Age wasn't the obstacle he'd imagined it would be. If anything, young girls appreciated his knowledge on top of his well-cared-for appearance. His winning records spoke for themselves.

They were drawn to his smiles. His lingering looks of assessment. He'd had that effect on Jeannine once. When he married her, he was sure he could bury memories of Annie, once and for all.

Wrong.

Striding across the field, he acknowledged the SUNY Cortland coach. "Your team looks great."

The coach shrugged. "A lot of miles to race before November." Teams milled around them, a kaleidoscope of color. Today's open invitational drew some top competition. Division One athletes rubbed shoulders with Division Three, and it would be anybody's race once the gun sounded. The Cortland coach watched his women take the line, then nodded to Tom. "You got anybody you want me to watch later?"

Baldwin shrugged. "Bittner, maybe. She'd fit your program. Strong, aggressive, a team player. No one outstanding this year, but I've got a youngster I'm priming."

"Too big and I lose them to Division One. Like Ellers."

"That girl could tool," Baldwin agreed.

Jackie Ellers. Brown sugar. Really photogenic. He'd gotten great shots. Her chocolate skin showed off the Forest Hills green. Nice contrast. Of course, her pictures didn't compare with Annie's. When Jackie's father returned from an overseas assignment, Tom realized the rugged African American was no one to trifle with. Jackie had been less than perfect, but things worked out. She'd padded his coaching stats and ended up going Division One, making him look real good.

"Ellers is one talented piece of work."

"As good as Kellwyn," noted another coach who'd moved alongside. "Not too many back woods coaches get that kind of talent, Baldwin, much less twice. You must be blessed."

Tom shrugged. "Or unusually good at developing young runners."

"You have a knack, that's for sure. But no one this year?"

"Nope. See me in twenty-four months. I've got some on-the-job-training to do."

Anne maneuvered her mother's wheelchair alongside the rope. Maura would only be able to see the start and finish, but the promise brought color to her cheeks. Her eyes shone with excitement. "This brings back memories, Anne," she crowed. "Good ones."

Anne nodded, but didn't agree. Her memories were mixed and she didn't want to drag them out. "Stay close," she warned Kyle as people pressed to see the start.

"Okay. The girls run first?"

"Today. Sometimes the guys do. They mix it up, give everyone a shot at an early or late race."

"Oh."

He looked bored. She ruffled his hair. "See that man?" She waited until he followed the direction of her finger. "He's going to fire a gun to start the race."

"Really?" His interest level rose. The prospect of nearly two hundred women vying for a title was small change compared to a man with a gun. Boys.

The shot erupted. Women surged forward, an array of color against the forest backdrop of fall trees and green grass. Multi-colored jerseys pushed by. Kyle watched, round-eyed, as the women juggled for placement. One stumbled, then fell, bringing down two others. Annie cringed. Starts were tough unless you were a top seed. Even then, nothing was guaranteed.

The women scrambled up and took off. Kyle grabbed Anne's hand. "Did they get hurt?"

"Just their pride, most likely. Come with me." She tugged him along. "Mom, we'll be right back. We're going to catch them at the bridge."

Her mother nodded. "I'll be right here."

Crossing the open field, Anne ran, Kyle's hand wrapped in hers, following a throng of people. Because cross-country was a natural landscape race, the runners wound through woods and fields, digging their way up hills and fighting spikes on pavement. A well-drawn path provided a mix, designed to challenge adaptability.

Anne had loved it. A private runner, she ran track out of necessity. Cross-country she ran for love. The wind on her face, messing her hair, pushing her on, tugging her back. The combination of elements, nature at its worst and best from September to November. She'd cherished every moment.

Moving west of the throng, she slipped into a more obscure clearing with Kyle. Here, the press of the crowd wouldn't block his view. Voices to her left told Anne the front-runners were approaching. "Watch, Kyle." Anne pointed. "Mind the rope, there. You don't want to get in the way of the runners."

He slipped into the opening and glanced back. "Is this okay?"

Anne nodded. "Perfect. The first girls to come through usually win. If you're not in the top five here, your chances of placing are pretty slim." She smiled as Kyle turned toward the oncoming noise.

"Not that you knew much about that, Annie."

Anne froze. The voice brought too many thoughts, too many memories. She darted a look to Kyle who was now several feet away, watching the leaders approach.

Stepping out from the tree line, Tom Baldwin stood between her and freedom. The charging front-runners blocked an exit to the woods. Kyle called, "Here they are, Mommy! The blue one's first."

She nodded, her throat tight, her heart racing. Baldwin stepped forward. "It's been a long time."

"Don't touch me."

The response was total gut. She stepped back, blocking Kyle. For the moment, he was mesmerized by the parade of thundering runners, oblivious to the confrontation behind him.

"You came back." Tom's eyes raked her, slow. Real slow. Her stomach clenched.

"Get out of here, Tom." She wanted a weapon, something hard and heavy. Sharp. She felt nothing but rope at her back, designed to keep spectators off the racecourse. Runners pounded past, the thud of feet like a cattle stampede through the narrowed creek crossing.

"You look good. Real good. Better, if possible." Tom's voice was slow. Contemplative. "I've missed you."

Anne sensed the pervading evil, although she couldn't discern Tom's face. He was backlit by the September sun, his body profiled in shadow.

But that voice had haunted her for too long. There'd be no forgetting that. "Come one step closer and I'll scream."

Her threat paused him. Remembering the wise words of her therapist, she forged on, her tone harsh but low, not wanting to upset Kyle. She actually took a step forward, so the boy wouldn't hear. "I'm not thirteen anymore, Tom. You put a hand on me, or threaten me in any way and I'll bring the law on you like that." She snapped her fingers in emphasis.

Kyle turned. "Mommy? Did you call me?"

Tom cocked his head, ignoring the boy. "The law as in Joe McIntyre? Won't find much help there."

That twisted her gut, but she refused to quake. "There's always the sheriff. And the state police. I saw one of their cruisers parked by the ambulance." She raised her chin. "They're not 'small town', Tom. They take complaints like this seriously."

His laugh didn't sound quite as certain as it had moments before. "You'd have done it long ago if you were going to. No." He shook his head, studying her. "The only place you were gutsy was on the race course. Or when you came on to me."

He noted her sharp inhale with a look of triumph. "You remember, don't you?" He nodded approval to her reaction. "You remember real well. Other than that, you were a mouse, hiding in holes." He stepped back. The sun lit his face then, and Anne was surprised to see he wasn't the monster of her memories. At five-nine and a runner's one-fifty, he was lean, not as intimidating as she remembered.

She grabbed Kyle's hand and drew him away, pushing through brush. Kyle offered protest at being pulled from the viewing spot. She ignored his complaints, needing to distance herself. She felt Tom's gaze as she moved, her body shielding Kyle, and it drew her back fifteen years.

A youngster, loving to run, eager to impress her renowned coach. A coach that reveled in being the local heart-throb. Tom had his own personal fan club. Flirtatious teens, playing a game of make-believe with a man who played for real. He'd picked her to run varsity, promising to guide her progress. He'd done it, too. By the time they ended the first summer's training, Anne found herself madly in love with a man twelve years her senior. He returned her affection with protracted looks. Affectionate hugs that lasted too long and led to warm, searing kisses. Touches. Promises. She'd been complimented, honored, beguiled.

How stupid can one girl get?

"Mommy, who was that man? Why don't we like him?" Kyle turned back, dismayed.

Anne stayed quiet, steering Kyle toward her mother. She felt Tom watching, his eyes piercing, but when she looked back, the forest line stood empty. Silent, she prayed, her breath staccato.

I can't do this, Lord. I can't. I haven't felt this pathetic in years. It scares me to think of the power he wields, the evil in him. I thought I was strong enough to handle this, but I'm not.

Help me, please. Show me what to do. I can't live scared again. I've come too far. I have my mother to think of. Not much time. I can't uproot her to avoid my past. But I can't face it, either.

Drawing close to her mother, she faked a smile and drew the light coverlet over her mother's lap. She waved a hand to the woods, drawing Kyle's attention. "The runners will come out there and circle to the finish line. Watch and see who comes out first."

"But—"

"But, nothing." Anne kept her voice firm. She didn't need Kyle to blurt something in front of her mother. She prayed that the combined noises had obscured Kyle's hearing. Some things a little boy just didn't need to know. She softened her tone and addressed him again. "Which one do you think will win?"

"Blue," voted Kyle, his tone decided.

"Could be." Anne nodded, willing her heart to slow. She brought her gaze back around to her mother. "How're we doing?"

Her mother cast her a sharp look. "Better than you. What's wrong?" She glanced at Kyle before bringing her eyes back to Anne's.

Anne shook her head. She didn't lie, but she didn't tell the truth, either. "Memories. They got to me, I guess." Refusing to meet her mother's eyes, she studied the field, watching for the front-runners. The last eight hundred meters was run in the open, a kicker's half-mile. The top-runners always brought the crowd surging with them, lining the ropes, cheering them in. The long loop would give Anne time to recoup.

Green against green. She made out Tom's form as he headed toward the athletic building. The same walk, same forward lean. She'd know that profile anywhere.

A hand touched her sleeve. Anne glanced down. Her mother's face showed concern. "What's going on?"

Shaking her head, Anne pointed to the woods, diverting attention. "Here's our winner."

Frowning, Maura turned, following the progress of a long-legged girl in white. She didn't appear to have a care in the world as she circled the east end of the field.

Then a flash of blue darted from the trees as a petite brunette with eggbeater legs barreled along.

"Mommy, look! It's the blue girl!" Obviously Kyle picked his favorites by color.

"Columbia," advised Anne, noting the girl's tenacity. Hearing the steps pounding behind her, the frontrunner tried to surge, but the momentum of the Columbia girl hurled her into first before the frontrunner recovered. She broke the tape, arms extended, almost setting a new course record. Anne grinned, remembering the feeling.

Maura pumped Anne's hand. "Wasn't that marvelous?" she crowed.

"Not if you're the one in white," supposed Anne, smiling.

"Blue won," crowed Kyle, jumping up and down. "She did it!"

As the crowd calmed, Anne leaned down. "How are you holding up?"

Maura's smile couldn't quite hide her weariness. "I've got enough energy for the men, then I need a nap."

"Reasonable enough," agreed Anne. "Joe is fixing the gutters so the basement dries out better. If the work's too noisy, I'll have him stop."

"It won't be if I take my hearing aid out."

Anne laughed. "True enough. Besides, now that he's working, we don't want to impede progress."

"He's gotten a lot done this past week," noted Maura.

"He had a lot to make up for," Anne shot back.

"Good point. But don't fight with him now. Let him finish, first."

Anne grinned. "I'll be the soul of discretion." Turning, another figure caught her eye. Bruce Kingston, moving toward them. She was caught between chagrin and guilt, but he seemed un-affronted to find her there.

"Beautiful day," he noted, drawing close. He nodded to Anne and stretched out a hand to her mother. "Bruce Kingston. I teach with Anne."

Maura smiled and shook his hand. "Maura Kellwyn." She nodded to Anne's left. "My grandson, Kyle."

"Nice to meet you, Kyle." Bruce put a steady hand on the boy's shoulder, then turned to Anne. "I thought I might find you here."

A flush heated her cheeks. "Mom hadn't been in a long while, so... We came."

He didn't mention she'd politely refused his invitation the day after he'd made the offer. "That Columbia girl's a whip, isn't she?"

"Yes." Running talk kept Anne on safe ground. She didn't try to examine why she'd refused Bruce's offer. It just hadn't felt right to say yes. "She's earning her berth on the 'A' team, no doubt."

"Well, that was an 'A' team performance." He watched the college guys jockey for position, shoulders cocked, hips angled, their chins tipped down, intent. He turned to catch her eye. "Does watching give you the urge to get back in the game?"

"I run for pleasure, now," she answered smoothly.

Not exactly true. She ran for pleasure but every part of her wanted to lead the pack. That little girl from Columbia wouldn't have stood a chance if Anne had been in the lead. Competing was part of her. A gift, a talent. She'd had big dreams, once. Thoughts of fame, Olympic gold.

But she'd canned them as self-degradation grew out of control. Instead she ran in other ways. Away from problems, from the fear of humiliation. Apprehensive of what that would have done to Joe, her husband. Pushing back thoughts of what could have been, she worked to steady shaky hands. *Help me, God.*

Bruce looked as if he didn't buy her answer, but nodded affably. "Shall we get some lunch when this is over?"

He had guts. She'd already turned him down once in private, and he still wasn't afraid to put it out there, in front of her mother and son.

Or was it a ploy to push her to say yes? Back her into a corner, and watch her struggle?

Meeting Tom brought out her dark side. She gave Bruce a kind look. "Mom's tired. I need to get her home after the men's race."

Bruce acquiesced easily. "Understandable. I'll help you to the car once the race is over. Have you thought about ways to channel more algebra into your science classes?"

"Uh, uh, Bruce." She shook her head, laughing. "Saturdays are my 'Kyle' day. No classroom talk allowed."

"He looks like you, Anne." Bruce smiled in Kyle's direction. "Except for the curls."

She shrugged. "Thanks. I see a lot of me in him." *Except he's braver,* she thought, watching the boy's excitement as the gun went off again. He didn't shirk or shrink back. She'd worked hard to encourage that, knowing the lack too well.

Joe shouldn't have swung the hammer once he heard her car. Accidents happened when a man's attentions were split. He strode into the garage scowling, shaking his hand.

"Are you hurt?"

He growled, grabbed a plastic gallon jug of tea and drank deeply, still shaking his left hand.

"You're such a bear, Joe."

He paused at her words. Stared.

She called him that, back in the day. He used to say that if he had an Indian name, it would be Bear. He would snap and growl for effect, most convincing. But she had a way of gentling him that would have made Teddy Roosevelt proud. He was a teddy bear in her arms, loving, anxious to please, sworn to protect.

He turned into a grizzly when she left.

It took a long while to ease down the Kodiak chain. Now, black bear, mostly. Fierce, but not as confrontational. Sometimes humorous, though he didn't have much to laugh at.

He sighed inside. Outwardly, he eyed her, his look cool. "How were the races?"

"Fine."

Wrong answer. False cheer. Maintaining a front. For him? Probably not. Then why?

He wondered in silence. Maybe her teacher friend hadn't been as much fun as she'd thought. Oh, he'd heard the invitation Kingston issued, and fought the feelings it stirred all week.

They'd been divorced for seven years. She was free to do whatever she chose. Legally, anyhow. Morally? The boy was proof positive she hadn't taken too long to figure that one out.

But it didn't help that his heart felt freshly stomped to know she'd borne someone else's child two years after dumping him, and was dating someone under his nose.

He quashed the anger as best he could. Not his business anymore. He angled his head to the back. "Can I show you something?"

"In a minute? I have to get Mom in for her nap."

"I'll help." Moving forward, he opened Maura's door, then reached out an arm. "May I?"

Maura turned her gaze to his.

Joe noted the difference right off. Her look of challenge had been exchanged for something softer. Searching. Well, that sure beat angry, accusatory, critical and confrontational.

"You may." Pushing up from the car, she leaned heavily on Joe. "I'm not a small woman," she reminded him, her voice tough, her eyes worn.

"Nothing I can't handle," he promised, keeping his arm taut. "And don't think I've forgotten what a toughie you are."

"Forgotten or ignored," she retorted, batting his arm with her loose one. Something flashed in her eyes, a message. He paused, not understanding. She gave him an impatient tug. "You're slower than you used to be."

"One of us is." Careful, he led her up the steps, wondering what inspired the look.

She'd refused to intervene when Anne disappeared, and barely spoke to him after. He'd come begging twice. Both times he'd left angrier than when he'd arrived. She shared no information and refused to pass anything on. "If Anne wants to talk to you, she'll contact you."

Joe never understood what he'd done to antagonize Maura Kellwyn. Sure she'd been nervous initially, when they started dating. Their age difference created talk, but he'd worked to win Maura over, show her his strength, his dependability.

But his gained ground vanished with Anne's desertion. All Maura would offer was that Anne chose a different path.

Right. A path that led to an advanced degree and an illegitimate child. Busy couple of years.

Going through the kitchen, Maura paused, working for breath. He stopped, letting her lean into his strength. As Anne clattered through the wooden door, Maura's voice beckoned him. "Joe..."

He leaned closer.

"We need..." she huffed for breath, trying to hurry, her voice strained, "to talk."

Joe pulled back. Her blue-gray eyes seemed sad. Despairing. What did she want, a last confession? He sighed, this time out loud, not wanting to be anyone's confessor. Least of all someone named Kellwyn. He nodded, but she didn't buy his half-hearted acceptance. Her hand squeezed his arm. "Soon. Alone."

Now he read the timeline in her eyes.

Of course. They always wanted to unload their sins when time grew short. *Why, God?* he lamented, leading her into the bedroom. *Why me? Why now? Why her, for heaven's sake?*

A part of him longed to turn her away like she'd done to him.

Joe was faithful enough to believe in a just God, but human enough to resent last minute efforts to right old wrongs. She gripped his arm as she sank to the mattress. "Please?"

He nodded as Anne stepped in to help her mother to the bathroom. As he backed out, Maura gave him one last look of entreaty.

Joe wanted to kick something. Anything.

His life had been settled. Full. He came and went as he chose, had a career he loved, a home he'd worked hard for. Well, not as hard as he should have, he chastised himself, looking around the rental that would take weeks to fix. Good thing he'd gotten his firewood in, or he'd be spending hunting season chopping wood. Now that would have made him mad. Nothing got in the way of shotgun season for whitetail.

Moving outside, he spied the boy using nature's facilities at the edge of the woods, and grinned as a voice rang out, "Kyle David, we have a bathroom for that."

"Grandma was using it, and I had to go *bad*," the boy protested, straightening his pants.

Joe worked to keep his face composed as Anne moved across the yard. "Go wash your hands," she ordered. She must have sensed Joe's empathy, because she swung his way. "And not a word from you."

He shook his head, fighting a smile as he climbed to the rear soffit.

She glared at him, then shut the kitchen door with a thump.

Okay. He probably wouldn't be showing her the new drainage system he'd worked out. Just as well. He bit his lip in concentration, averting his gaze from the tightly closed entry. At least he wouldn't have to worry about the hammer strikes waking the old woman. She looked like she needed rest and plenty of it, and would find eternal rest sooner rather than later.

How would Anne handle that, he wondered. To have given up her job and her life to help out, only to lose her mother within months.

She'd be devastated, he realized. His parents were much younger than Anne's. Jim and Deb McIntyre had been high school sweethearts, and for a while it seemed like he was destined to a similar end with Annie.

But, no. His parents had lived and loved for nearly thirty-six years, with a faith in God and one another that seemed rare nowadays. Salt of the earth, good people. Devoted.

His six months didn't hold a candle.

By the time he finished applying the gutters, the light had faded. He stowed his tools and tapped on the door. Anne answered, her face set. "I'm done for today," he told her. He tugged his cap into place and nodded to his SUV. "I'm working tonight, so I've got to get to the office. Your mom okay?"

Realization softened her features. "You're going to work now?"

"Well, once I get home and shower. Change my clothes. Sure. We rotate weekend nights. That way no one's always put out."

She shook her head, embarrassed. "I'm sorry. I didn't realize." Her lips pursed. "Are you hungry? Can I fix you a sandwich?"

The makings of a Saturday night supper lay behind her. Sub rolls, meats, cheeses. A garden tomato, fresh-sliced. Italian dressing from the specialty store in Watertown. His mouth watered, but his heart hardened. "I'll grab something in town. I won't be back 'til Monday. I'll need to sleep tomorrow, after church."

"Of course you will," she exclaimed, sounding troubled. "Will you be all right, Joe?"

He frowned, not understanding.

"Going into work after all you've done here," she pressed. "Will you be okay? Stay awake?"

Something stirred inside him. A tiny flame, fanned by the worry in her voice. He took firm hold of an equally virtual fire hose and doused the flicker of heat with gallons of pretend water. Talk about overkill. "Nothing new or different in that. Good night." He tipped his cap.

For just a moment, concern showed on her face, her brow drawn. Then she composed herself, stepping back, those hazel eyes shuttered against emotion. "Good night."

CHAPTER 9

The front page of the Canton-Potsdam Herald wondered if Tom Baldwin had found another one.

Anne's mug rattled as she set it down, reading without wanting to.

"Tom Baldwin, renowned coach of the Forest Hills running programs, whose Class D wins strike fear in the hearts of similarly-sized schools across the state, may have another protégé.

"Missy Volmer," the reporter continued, *"an eighth grade running sensation, is moving to the varsity squad after successfully passing the state's criteria for performance above grade level."*

"'Missy', boasts Coach Baldwin, 'whose specialty appears to be middle-distance, will be a fine addition to the already strong women of Forest Hills. I'm looking forward to the opportunities coaching her will provide.'

Baldwin's current record is 3-1-1, with a bitter loss to arch-rival Campbell Springs last week."

Anne's stomach twisted. Her eyes darted back, catching one phrase repeatedly. *"...looking forward to the opportunities coaching her will provide."*

He couldn't possibly mean—?

No. It couldn't be. There weren't others, were there? Tom was married, with three children. Why would he risk losing everything?

The possibility of other victims made her silence worse, allowing a predator to go unchecked. She understood Tom. His aura, his presence. The way he could look at a girl and make her think she was special.

She gripped the table, trying to rein in emotion.

She pictured Tom befriending her, laughing with her, flirting with her. He snapped picture after picture, catching her mid-stride, talking of her future, their future, the excitement of it all. Having her shed her warm-ups, toss them aside, the camera shutter clacking...

Did she comprehend the consequences of her actions then? No. No way. She was a baby, thirteen years old, filled with a young girl's dreams of ever after. How could she have been so foolish?

She'd been through this with her therapist. God bless Melissa, she'd laughed and cried with Anne, helping her to realize that children are victims, not partners. Except that Anne could never fully erase those feelings of guilt. Of enjoying Tom's attentions, and yes, his touch. Nope. She couldn't quite forgive herself that, despite understanding physiological function. She'd made choices and paid for them. End of story.

The school bell chimed. Anne startled back into the present.

What should she do? There he was, pictured in the notable green that represented Forest Hills, his smile bright while he talked of opportunities provided by an eighth grade girl.

God, help me. I don't know how to handle this. Who to turn to. I've come so far from where I was, and I don't want to get involved, but I can't let this happen to someone else.

Doubts assailed her. An inner voice played devil's advocate.

Maybe you were the only one. That makes it you against him, Anne. Who are they going to believe? A woman with a grudge against a town that shunned her, or a man who garners wins with never a complaint lodged against him?

"I don't know," she whispered, cornered.

"Anne?"

She jerked up. Bruce stood in the doorway of the lounge. He stepped forward, worried. "Are you okay?"

She nodded, backing up.

"You're white as a ghost," he insisted, following her. "Sit down."

"I can't." She used the clock as an excuse. "I have class." Darting past him, she hurried down the hall, heart pounding.

Feelings swarmed her. Guilt, anger, fear, frustration. *Now would be good, God,* she prayed fervently. *I've got twenty-two kids who need me to be coherent. Get me through today, please. Then we'll talk again.* She paused outside her classroom, shutting her eyes.

The hall had emptied. To her surprise, her class sat quiet, no spitballs or erasers being tossed.

Like a mid-summer breeze, peace coursed through her. A touch, feather-light. Almost tangibly, the burdens lifted from her shoulders. Her body relaxed into itself once more. *Thank you, Father.* She breathed the words then walked into the room, shoulders back, head high.

"You're not yourself tonight." Maura pushed aside her untouched tapioca pudding, one of her favorites. "What's wrong?"

"Just tired."

"No."

Anne glanced over from where she graded papers. "I'm not allowed to get tired?" She put a hint of amusement in her voice.

"Allowed, yes. But it's more than that. I've been your mother for nearly thirty years, Annie-Lou. I know when something's eating at you."

But you didn't, thought Anne, lowering her eyes. *I hid everything so well that even you didn't know, Mom. What good would it do for you to find out now? How would that make you feel, while the angels gather in escort? I'm supposed to dump fifteen years of guilt on you? Not going to happen.*

Anne met her mother's look of concern. "I am tired," she repeated, steadying her voice. "But I'm also worried, knowing how sick you are and wishing I could do more. Be here more."

"The girls that come in take good care of me," Maura protested, "and the visiting nurse stops every morning. I'm not at crisis point yet."

Well... Not exactly true. They both knew that the end could be a gradual slowing or a quick stoppage. There were no predictors, but Anne refused to argue the point. "Good thing. I'm not ready to say goodbye."

"You need to get ready then." Her mother's voice was soft but earnest.

Anne moved to her mother's side and clasped her hand. "Are you in pain?"

Her mother shook her head. "No. Just awful tired. It's soon, Anne, I can feel it. Now don't cry," she protested, reaching a frail hand to caress Anne's cheek. "There's plenty of time for tears later. I want this time to be happy."

Her voice seemed stronger. Her thin-skinned fingers feathered soft against Anne's face. Maura puckered her lips, studying her daughter. "Something eats at you, Anne. All these years, I thought it was Joe. That he'd done something to hurt you. But it wasn't Joe you ran from, was it?"

Anne's chest convulsed. She fought a sob. Biting her lower lip, she tightened her hands. "I don't know what you mean."

Maura eyed her. "You do," she decided long seconds later. "You know exactly what I mean, but you don't want to burden me. How much worse that is, Anne, knowing you're hiding something to protect me. Don't," she begged, her hand stroking Anne's cheek. "I don't need protection now. I need to see God with my heart whole, my soul purged."

"Mom." Tears slipped out, uncontrolled. "I can't." Thoughts of the time past, the fear and guilt, mounted. She looked down. "It's nothing I can't handle. You've got enough on your plate."

Maura grasped Anne's chin. "Will you run again?"

Anne cringed. "Most likely."

"From what?" When she didn't answer, her mother asked again. This time her voice was deep with restrained anger. "Who hurt you, Annie? Tom Baldwin?"

Anne jerked up. She stared at her mother, mouth open. Maura read the look and sank back. Her face twisted in remorse.

"Mom—"

"I knew it," her mother breathed, her voice small but fierce. "The minute you came out of the woods with him following, I knew it. All that while," she lamented, growing more agitated, "I assumed you ran from Joe. I looked at your sadness and your fear, and thought he must be hurting you. Oh, Anne." Her mother's jaw trembled, then firmed. "I would have protected you from anything, Anne. But I didn't, did I?" Her eyes wet, she sought Anne's hand in comfort. "I didn't protect my little girl, and look what's come of it."

"I'm fine, Mom." Anne struggled to control her voice. "I'm grown up, able to fight my own battles. Face the demons. Don't worry about something that happened fifteen years ago. It's over. Done."

Maura's face blanched. "Fifteen years." Her breathing accelerated. "Anne, you were..."

"Thirteen," Anne supplied, her tone tight. "A long time ago, Mom. There's no time for recriminations now. I've dealt with it, put it behind me."

"Coming back must have been torture for you." Maura's voice weakened. Her expression reflected the horror of her newfound knowledge, exactly why Anne didn't want her to know. What was the point?

"No." Anne shook her head, swiping the backs of her hands to her cheeks. "Coming back was good. Kyle and I've had a chance to be with you. Nothing's more important than that. Mom," she kissed her mother's cheek, then grasped the old woman's hands. "You weren't responsible for what happened then. I was," Anne admitted, glancing away. Breathing deep, she brought her gaze back to her mother's. "I thought I was in love with him."

"You were a child, Anne." Maura sputtered, tightening her grip. "He was a grown man. A teacher and a coach." Her eyes searched Anne's as she tried to make sense of this revelation. "You weren't responsible for his depraved actions."

Anne studied the carpet. "I went off alone with him. He wanted to take some pictures. He said he was going to submit them to magazines. Keep a file. I hammed it up, good," she confessed.

Her mother nodded, her clasp snug. "And then?"

Anne gnawed her lip. "He kissed me. Told me he wanted me. Needed me." A tear dropped to her lap, then another. She sniffled and shook her head. "I believed him. How stupid I was." She studied their entwined hands, frowning. "He kept saying he loved me. Needed to be with me. And I thought it was so romantic. So beautiful. And then..."

"Come here." Maura pulled Anne closer, cradling her daughter's head. "Why didn't you tell us? We could have helped you. Had him arrested. There are laws against things like this. You were a baby, no matter what you thought. That's why there are laws against sex between minors and adults."

"I was thirteen," Anne reminded her, the feel of her mother's cotton wrap soft against her cheek. "Not a baby."

"When it comes to matters like that, you were still a child." Her mother's voice went no nonsense. "No normal man preys on children. He needs to pay for what he's done, Anne. He needs to atone for his sin."

"And me for mine."

"Annie." Maura rubbed Anne's back with a firm touch. "Why didn't you tell me? I would have helped. You know that."

Anne fought the threatening sob. The pull of emotion reached up to wrack her. Her shoulders shuddered. Maura held tight. "Why?"

Anne lifted her face. "Because it was the day Daddy died."

Maura's eyes widened. She drew a deep, shuddering breath. "No."

Anne nodded, revealing the truth. "While Tom and I were tangled in the woods, Daddy took his last breaths. Calling for me. And I wasn't here."

"Oh, baby." Maura's tears joined Anne's. She clutched Anne closer. "Dear Lord, help us. Help us, please. Forgive me, Jesus, for not seeing the pain my daughter was in, for not sheltering her from a beast like Tom Baldwin."

"No, Mom. No." Anne drew back, fear for her mother's heart condition taking precedence. "It wasn't your fault. It was mine."

"It wasn't," Maura shot back. "You can't blame yourself for this, Anne. It's wrong. He was the adult, the perpetrator. Not you."

Melissa had said the same thing, but the words rang strong coming from her mother. Anne pulled tissues from the box and plied them to her eyes and nose. "I had a crush on him, Mom. I thought I loved him. I even had dreams about him. If I'd shown better sense—"

"Nonsense." Her mother interrupted her with a look of amazement. "Half the kids in school get crushes on their teachers. You think that's unusual, that it makes you bad? Ridiculous, Annie."

Her mother's staunch tone raised Anne's sense of hope.

"You're a teacher. What if one of your eighth grade boys was attracted to you? Would you take him into the woods and have sex with him?"

"Of course not." Anne bristled. "They're kids." She said it as if the time frame made the answer obvious.

"Exactly." Maura tipped Anne's chin to gaze into her eyes. "You weren't responsible for what happened. Not in the least. And then to come home and find out your Daddy died." Her voice trailed off. Once more she grabbed Anne into her arms. "Oh, my poor, sweet, girl. My beautiful girl. What a horrible day that was."

"I wanted to tell him goodbye," Anne whispered, no longer trying to thwart the tears. They ran, unchecked, wetting her mother's robe. "To say how much I loved him. And all because I—"

"He knew, honey." Maura interrupted, pressing her cheek against Anne's hair. "He always knew. You showed him in so many ways. He had dreams for you. You made them all come true, Annie-Lou, and he'd be very proud of his beautiful daughter."

"Not of everything." Anne moved beyond sugarcoating the obvious. She'd piled mistake upon mistake. Sin on sin. White-out didn't work on that kind of grievous error.

> "'Before I was afflicted I went astray: but now have I kept thy word,'" her mother quoted. "'Thou art good, and doest good; teach me thy statutes. The proud have forged a lie against me: but I will keep thy precepts with my whole heart.' From the Psalms, Annie. The Lord forgives. You know that."

Unconvinced, Anne frowned. Maura shook her head. "You need to forgive yourself. The Lord has already wiped the slate clean. Don't doubt His good judgment." After a moment's thought, she sharpened her gaze. "Is this why you ran from Joe, Annie?" She narrowed her eyes, puzzled. "You left because you felt guilty about Tom?"

Anne drew a deep breath. "Tom threatened to expose me as a little tramp who lost her virginity in eighth grade."

Maura grabbed Anne's hand. "But that would have revealed his part in it." Her frown deepened. "I don't understand."

"Blackmail, pure and simple. He wanted me at his beck and call." Her arched brow told Maura what that meant. "He sent pictures he'd taken that first day. They made it look like I was flirting with him. He told me to cooperate, or the next pictures would go to Joe, and there'd be no need to explain those."

"Oh, Annie." Maura's expression saddened. "You could have told Joe, honey. He would have understood."

"Would he?" Anne thought of Joe's pride in their relationship. They'd come to each other untouched, or so he thought. He'd waited for her to be his wife to enjoy the pleasures of the marriage bed, and then had loved her with every ounce of his being. "I'm not so sure. I may have been young, but I was part of the problem."

"You weren't," her mother insisted, adamant. "You need to take this to God. It's not right, you accepting blame for Tom's lust. His depravity. His actions weren't normal, despite how you thought you felt."

Her mother's righteousness bolstered Anne. She drew a breath. "I'll try. I really will."

Anne hoped she sounded more certain than she felt. Today's article planted disturbing ideas into her head. Knowing Tom's gift for innuendo, it would be like him to brag using hidden meanings. He'd consider that a victory.

But she couldn't deal with that now. Right now she needed to calm her mother. "I love you, Mom. I couldn't have asked for better parents."

Maura cried without spilling tears. The medications had dried more than her mouth. Annie hugged her. "Stop. Please. It's all right."

"We didn't have much, Anne."

"We had plenty," Anne corrected. "Remember what Daddy used to say? 'Enough is as good as a feast.' I believe that, Mom. We don't need overmuch. Just enough. You always gave me that, and more. Look at the weekends you gave up, going to races, piling miles onto those old cars." She smiled, remembering.

"Are there good memories, Anne? Mixed in?"

Anne nodded. "Most of them. Coming back's been good for me, pushing me to face the past. That should help me move on. I just wish I'd had the courage before you got sick."

"God leads us, child. He brought you back when you were strong enough to handle it. His timing is perfect."

The timeline hadn't felt all that perfect. She swept her mother's dry cheek a kiss. "I don't want you beating yourself up. I should have told you long ago, but I was ashamed, and we were both so sad at losing Daddy."

Maura leaned back. "We need to talk more of this," she decided, her voice stronger.

Anne couldn't agree. What good would it do to talk the thing to death?

"He can't get away with this, Anne. He assaulted you. I can't believe he's gotten away with it this long."

"Who would believe me?" Anne whispered. "My word against Tom's, fifteen years later? For years people witnessed how good he was to me. That's what they'll remember, Mom. The thought is ludicrous."

"Right is right, Anne," declared the old woman. "There's no room for excuses."

Anne pushed up, pressing her lips in consternation. She stood silent, contemplating. "I'll think about it."

"Pray, Anne. He won't lead you astray." Her mother's eyes went skyward.

"I know." Although in agreement, she tightened her brow as thoughts coursed through her head, remembering how the locals had treated her for dumping Joe. How would they treat a woman who accused their beloved coach of pedophilia? They'd go for the jugular, and that meant they'd ferret out Kyle's birth and press her unmarried state. She shook her head, confused. "I have to think of Kyle, too. What something like this would do to him."

"What does running teach him?" Her mother looked suddenly drained. "We'll pray," she decided, her voice softening. She reached for Anne's hand, squeezing lightly. "Our Father, Who art in heaven. Hallowed be Thy name..."

"Thy kingdom come, Thy will be done, on Earth as it is in heaven..."

They prayed with measured pace, the lyrical words rising. When Maura finally drifted to sleep, Anne considered the verse from Matthew. *Where two or more are gathered in My name...*

Are You here, God? Do you hear our plea?

What should she do? Go public? Air the soiled linens?

Yes, if it meant saving someone from a similar fate. How could she do less?

But the thought of the aftermath stalled her. Her mother, already weakened. How much strain could an old woman bear?

And Kyle, so innocent. The conditions of his birth would be laid out in court if they got that far. She knew enough about rape cases to understand she would be scrutinized, her life an open book.

Would it matter that she was young and foolish? Perhaps not when the judge and jury looked at those pictures, happily posed. Anne in her warm-ups, Anne removing her warm-ups. The skimpy singlet in classic Forest Hills green. Spandex briefs stretched tight as Anne modeled exercises along the split rail fence adjacent to the old hunting cabin. A one shoulder shot, her smile coquettish as she gazed into the lens. A lot could be made of those.

Sleep was a long time coming. When it did, old dreams haunted. A mix of images, in jigsaw fashion. Joe and Kyle, hopeful, expectant. Her mother, happy and sad. Tom Baldwin, his slow, lethal smile haunting her sleep. And always in the background, a young girl running, her green warm-ups dancing through the trees.

"Did your mom have a rough night?" Joe eyed Anne the next morning as he lifted a ladder from the boot of his SUV.

She frowned. "No. Why?" Moving forward, she tucked her teaching bag into the back of the Civic.

"Because you look beat."

"Thanks." She huffed a breath into the chill October air. Already the frost had snuffed all but the hardiest flowers under the trees and along the porch. The trees were near peak. Soon, they'd be bare. Stark.

"Look, I just meant—"

"It's all right." Her voice said nothing was all right. She didn't look his way as she climbed into the car, then backed down the drive, avoiding the side of his SUV.

Joe hoisted the ladder, shaking his head. Why did he try? He didn't want to be nice to Anne, or kind to her mother, or teach someone else's son about turtles, mice, velociraptors and women. He had his own life, his own responsibilities. He'd kept them minimal for just that reason, to ensure his chance for normalcy.

He glared at his watch. He had two hours here, before a court appearance in Potsdam, then a full day's work.

The least she could do was be civil.

By the time he'd scraped and primed the front of the house, he'd cooled off. Anne had never been a morning person. He knew that. The idea of making conversation with her when she walked out of the house looking pretty but vulnerable had bumbled his tongue. What did he care if she looked beautiful or tired? Not a whit.

The fact that she looked both disturbed him. It meant she'd had too much practice being tired and worn.

But that was her business, not his. She'd made sure of that a long time ago.

The front door banged as Kyle hurried out, his backpack slapping his knee. "Hey, Joe."

"Hey, Bud." He inclined his head. "Off to school?"

"Yes." The boy shook with excitement. "It's library day and I can get a new book. If I get another one on dinosaurs, will you read with me?"

No, Joe wanted to shout. *Stop bothering me. Get your old man to read you stories, kid. Leave me...*

Joe bit back the thoughts. Keeping his eye on the brush loaded with oil-based primer, he gave a nod he didn't feel. "I can fit that in."

"Thanks." The boy's grin nearly split his face. His tousled head bobbed. Joe groaned inside. "Tonight?"

Joe shook his head. "Gotta work tonight, Buddy. Tomorrow night, okay?" He could finish painting after work, then read to the boy. He narrowed his eyes, thinking. That would work.

"Okay." The bus lumbered into view. Kyle ran down the drive, waving excitedly. "Bye, Joe."

"See ya, Bud."

A horn tooted as the bus rolled to a stop. "That you, Joe?"

Wonderful. The day couldn't get better, and only seven-forty-five. Marion Jenkins, the fastest tongue north of Watertown, waggled fingers at him through the windshield. Didn't it figure? He waved back, angling his head from his perch on the ladder. "Morning, Marion."

"Looks good, Joe. See you got an early start," she crowed through the open door.

Uh huh. No doubt she can't wait to inform the world that I was parked in Annie's driveway at first light. Great. Just great. "Gotta make use of the light," he called back. "Have a good day, now."

"Well, I will," she answered. He heard the speculation in her voice. He'd made her day, giving her something to gnaw on at the transportation garage. Oh, well. If it hadn't been her, it would have been someone else.

He toyed with the idea of seeing Anne's mother. The old woman had insisted on talking to him. He wasn't looking forward to the one-on-one, but he'd given his word.

A glance at his watch forestalled the idea. He was due at the county courthouse before he relieved Kim. He'd sneak time with her the next evening, he decided, lowering the ladder so Kyle wouldn't be tempted into roof adventures. Something about kids and ladders made the combination irresistible.

"Hear you're fixing up your property on Old Orchard," Boog noted as he examined the beveled edge of a cabinet door later that afternoon.

"Needed work." Joe examined a miniature birdhouse, then noted the carved dinosaur to its right. "How long do you think it takes Hi to make these?"

Boog shrugged. "He's got nothing but time with Myra gone. Just him and the wood."

Boog consigned products to augment his own creations for his Main Street shop. Hi Evers, from up river, made an artistry of carving creatures. Boog jerked a shoulder to the back of the store. "Whole display over there. I plan to move it up front this week, do a window display. Get ready for Christmas."

"In October?"

"Fourth quarter," noted Boog. "People are getting back to buying quality gifts. Enduring."

"Yeah. LCD TVs and satellite dishes."

Boog slanted a glance to the front of the store. "You think any more about that rocker?"

"Thought about my chair," rejoined Joe, ignoring the bait. He headed toward Hi's display. "How's it coming?"

"Still down the list," acknowledged the woodcrafter. "But you'll have it in time for your holiday dinner."

"Thanksgiving?"

"Thought you ate that at your mother's." At Joe's grin, Boog relaxed. "Christmas. You don't hurry the wood. A smart man works with the grain, not against. Saves time and aggravation."

Joe hoisted a carved dinosaur, then flipped it over to check the price. He whistled. "No wonder Hiram likes to carve."

"Worth every cent."

Joe nodded, eyeing the workmanship of the scaled down raptor. "Yes, it is. I'll take it."

"Starting a dinosaur collection?"

"Always liked them." Rolling out his money, Joe placed two twenties on the counter. "You got a bag for this?"

"I do."

With the bag tucked under his arm, Joe strode to the door, but not before caressing the planes of the hard-maple rocker.

Boog had placed the chair near the stove. He'd draped a quilt across the back. Not too big, not too thick. Just right for drawing over your lap on a cold, northern night. The quilt reminded Joe of Anne, soft blues, greens and browns on an ivory background. On the chair seat sat a child's doll, a bit tousled, as if left, mid-story.

The scene said home. Family. Scented wood burning in the grate, toes curled in quiet satisfaction. Joe trailed one finger along the honeyed grain, then turned, shielding his emotions. He hoisted the bag. "Thanks, Boog. I'll be around."

Boog kept his eyes on his work, his expression mellow. "Always a pleasure, Chief."

CHAPTER 10

"Joe's gonna read this to me tomorrow," Kyle announced, flashing the large-scaled dinosaur book to his mother and grandmother.

"He is?"

"Uh huh." Kyle nodded. "I asked him this morning. He said he was busy tonight, but he'd read to me tomorrow."

"You shouldn't bother him, Kyle," Anne protested.

"Why?" Kyle wondered. "He said okay."

"Of course he did." Anne fumbled for a reason and grasped the old stand-by. "He's busy, honey."

"Well, he said all right," answered Kyle as if that was that.

"Doesn't hurt the boy to have a man around," chimed Maura.

"But it could," Anne asserted. Having Kyle grow attached would be a mistake. Just one more thing to give up when they moved on. "How's your tea, Mom?"

"Just right." She'd barely sipped it.

Anne smiled. "Good. Would you like more?"

Her mother met Anne's smile with one of her own. They recognized one another's efforts at normalcy. Maura nodded to Kyle. "I'll read to you."

"Really?" He sounded surprised.

She nodded. "Sure. I can still see. I just don't breathe so well anymore."

Kyle eyed the nasal oxygenator. "I'm glad that machine helps, Grandma."

She settled the boy alongside, allowing him to hold one half of the book while she anchored the other. "Me, too."

Anne wasn't sure what woke her. Instinct? The presence of celestial beings? A blanketing silence? Crossing to her mother's room, she felt the change right off. Switching on the brighter light, she noted the gray pallor of her mother's lips. The unnatural paling of her fingernails. "Mom?"

Maura's breaths were short. Shallow. Almost non-existent. Trying not to panic, Anne dialed nine-one-one.

"Chief, I know you're not on, but we just got a call to your ex-wife's house. I think her mom's calling it a night."

Joe jumped out of bed. "I'll head right over." Rushing, he wasn't sure why he felt the need. Maura Kellwyn hadn't helped his cause over the years. Yeah, she'd been an okay tenant. Better than that, actually, considering she hadn't complained about his lack of interest in her surroundings.

But something about the look she'd offered him the other day had him curious. Wondering. What on earth could she want to say after so much time?

And maybe not enough time, thought Joe as he sped downhill. The eight minutes from his A-frame to Maura's rental could be enough to spell the end.

The ambulance arrived just before he did, along with the customary police escort. Mike Flanigan watched as Joe careened onto the side of the road, shoving the Explorer into low before it came to a complete stop. Nodding to his officer, Joe strode into the house, feeling pushed to hurry.

He saw the boy first. Through the hustle and bustle of the paramedics, Kyle stood to the side, his lower lip outthrust. “Hey, Buddy.”

He turned. Seeing Joe, he launched himself into his arms. Joe scooped him up, using his big frame to anchor the child. Feeling the chill of Kyle’s skin, he grabbed a knitted throw and cocooned the boy. “Best to stay warm, Bud. Cold is cold up here.”

Kyle nodded, easing into Joe’s chest. “That’s what Mommy says.”

Joe knew that. Hadn’t he heard it often enough? He watched as decisions were made in the bedroom beyond. There was a flurry of arms and jumbled talk, then Clyde Ritchie motioned him over. “She wants you.”

Joe looked behind him, then swung back to Clyde. “Who? Me?”

“You still Joe McIntyre?” the ambulance attendant growled.

“Yeah, but...” Joe thought hard. “Why does...”

“There’s not much time.” Anne slipped through the door, reaching for Kyle. Her calm sounded forced. “Let’s go say good-bye, big guy.”

Joe handed her the boy. Chilled air swept his skin as the child’s warm body left his. Quiet, he followed Anne into the familiar room, his eyes drawn to the prone figure.

Not much time was right. The breaths, faint and growing further apart, sped up as Maura struggled to open her eyes. “Joe.”

Joe stepped forward. Interested eyes watched his progress until he turned and slid his gaze to the door. “Give us a minute.”

No one dared argue. Respecting the old woman’s right to die in peace, the responders filed into the kitchen. Once they’d gone, Joe walked to the upper edge of the bed and leaned down. “I’m here.”

Maura grasped his arm with a surprisingly strong grip. "Psalm fifty-one," she whispered, laboring. "It wasn't you," she continued, her voice almost too small to be heard. He had to put his ear right to her lips to make out the words. Leaning back, he searched her eyes. "I thought it was." A low moan escaped her as she struggled to speak.

"It's all right," Joe offered, unsure what he was excusing. He'd sort out her confusing statements later. For the moment, he hated to see the old woman use her last strength on him while Anne huddled nearby. "It's okay."

"All this time," Maura whispered, her hand flexing his thick flannel. "I'm sorry."

Her struggling voice droned. He grasped her hand, his touch gentle. "Don't worry about it. Everything's fine. Annie's right here. With Kyle." Stepping back, he gave her hand another reassuring squeeze before backing away.

It was impossible not to feel sorry for her at this moment, regardless of their history. He swiped a hand across his brow, contemplating her words. *"It wasn't you."*

What wasn't him?

"I thought it was. All this time."

What had she thought? She was sorry for how she'd treated him? A little late, wasn't it? He backed away, watching as Anne's lips moved, her voice soft. She leaned over, and Joe's eyes filled as the boy pressed a kiss to Maura's cheek.

"Bye, Grandma. I love you."

Kyle's heartfelt words racked Anne's self-control. Her throat constricted and her lips pressed out. Joe stepped forward and reached for the boy so Anne could say her own goodbyes.

She grasped her mother in a comforting hug and murmured loving reassurance as the breaths faded. Paused.

For long seconds the room held no sound except for the burbling whir of the oxygenator. Slowly, Anne straightened. Leaning over, she hit a small button, plunging the room into silence. Kyle started at that.

"Why is it so quiet, Mommy?" The tremble in his voice reflected an understanding beyond his years.

Anne turned, but the words wouldn't come. Joe placed a gentle hand across the grandmother's face, shutting eyes that now saw beyond earth's constricting planes. "Grandma's gone home to heaven, Bud."

"Mommy?"

Reaching out, Anne took Kyle, enveloping him in her arms, tears flowing unrestrained.

Joe wanted to hold her.

The very thought made him mad enough to forego the notion. Here she was, after eight years of complete and utter silence, weaseling her way into his heart because of a sad little kid and an old woman's deathbed confession. One that made no sense.

But then, it had been a long time since he'd been able to say he understood the Kellwyn women.

Still, Anne's grief encompassed him. He couldn't watch her hold the boy, her tears wetting the child's hair and cheek, and not hold her. Comfort her.

He should leave.

Clenching his jaw, he moved toward the door that separated the grieving from the idly curious.

"Mommy? Are you okay?"

Kyle's voice turned him around. A rough road for a kid who'd only been here a short while, to have to say good-bye a few months later.

At the boy's words, Anne's shoulders shook harder. She tried to nod.

Joe wanted to swear. Really wanted to. Not just little bad words, either. All the big, nasty, shock your mother into total embarrassed silence bad words he'd ever heard in thirty-four years of North Country life came to mind.

He held them in check, figuring he'd duke it out with the Holy Spirit later. Why was he the one asked to be in attendance? What purpose was there in witnessing Maura's death, the boy's confusion and Anne's breakdown?

The old woman had quoted a psalm number. Fifty-one. He'd read that one often in the past, as anger and pride threatened to overtake him. "The sacrifice you want is a broken spirit. A broken and repentant heart, O God, You will not despise."

Feeling the words penetrate his soul, he stepped forward, arms out, enveloping mother and son in the safety of his embrace, trying not to notice how good and right it felt to hold Anne Kellwyn again.

CHAPTER 11

Joe's mother stepped into the living room of their hunters' lodge, dressed for the funeral. Joe eyed her. "You're coming?"

She looked surprised. "Of course. Anne was a part of this family. I have nothing against her or her mother."

"Except that she left me without a word for eight long years." The emotions of the past seventy-two hours were catching up with him. That, and lack of sleep.

The look Deb McIntyre sent him saw a little too much. "Perhaps she might have assumed you'd gotten over it by now. Moved beyond."

"I moved beyond a long time ago," he retorted. "Her being here just..." He stopped and shrugged.

"Brings everything back?"

"Yeah."

"Have you talked with her?" His mother asked, curious. "Asked her anything?"

"Like why she did it?" Joe snorted. "Not and gotten any kind of answer."

"But you did talk to her?" Deb pressed.

"I tried. It wasn't pretty."

"You've been angry for a long time," noted his mother. "I bet it wasn't."

Joe's father and brother came down the stairs as Joe headed for the door.

"How's Anne getting to the church?" his mother asked.

Joe shook his head. "I don't know. I offered a ride. She refused. I'll see you there." Moving out the door, he turned a blind eye to the exchange of looks behind him.

Watching Joe leave, Jim McIntyre shook his head. "I don't know how he could still be interested in her, Deb. After all this time? What she did to him? Why would he?"

"Because they were meant for each other," she replied. "They've got unfinished business. My guess would be that Anne's gone through a sight more than Joe."

"How do you figure?" Jim raised his chin in Joe's defense.

Deb handed him her coat. He helped her slip it on. "It's in her face. The way she walks, the way she talks. The girl's an open book for anyone who knows how to read."

"I can read," her husband declared. "I read the sports section every day."

"And Field and Stream," offered Greg, teasing. "Reader's Digest."

Deb gave the newly licensed doctor a friendly swat. "Don't help him," she warned. "If a situation fails to involve a cleat, gun or fishing lure, your father tends toward oblivion."

Jim drew her in and planted a kiss on her mouth. "Not totally," he reminded her, smiling into her eyes.

She shook her head, but answered his smile with one of her own. "No. Not totally." She felt her cheeks tinge pink with the look he sent her. Thirty-five years of marriage and the man could still make her blush by meeting her gaze. Dropping a wink.

Not bad, all in all.

Sally Mort drove Anne and Kyle to the church. Joe waited in the back, his family already seated.

Anne appeared sad but composed. She'd opted for a long skirt, and he knew from experience how cold the hillside graveyard would be with the north wind kicking. He was glad she had a full-length coat. The flash of red in the scarf around her neck added warmth to the somber look of black coat, boots and gloves.

She turned. Met his gaze. A look flashed between them, a mix of old angst and new awareness. Joe felt the intensity of the moment to his core.

He took a step back, mentally and physically. Her vulnerability was getting to him. Weakening his defenses. He'd been there before. It was no place he wanted to go again. Giving her the kind of polite commiseration the police chief would offer any grieving constituent, he inclined his head, then walked inside.

Nodding to the few mourners in attendance, Joe slipped into the pew occupied by his family. His mother glanced across the aisle to where Anne would sit, then gave him a look of interest.

He ignored her lack of subtlety.

As the service commenced, Joe noted the mourners. Sally Mort sat to Anne's right, with Kyle nestled on the left. Maura's next-door neighbors were there. A few old women from the church sat just behind them. They used to quilt with Maura, until varying ailments kept them side-lined. Tom Baldwin and his wife sat a few pews back. Bruce Kingston, of course, with the Redmond High principal. Not many, but enough. Anne could draw her support from the likes of them. Joe was fresh out.

By the time they'd completed the graveside service, Joe had reconsidered. Anne looked done in and it wasn't quite noon. Seeing her waver, he had no intention of letting her faint in front of the small crowd. As the minister closed his book of prayer, Joe eased behind her. At the same time, Tom Baldwin approached from the other side, facing Anne, his wife flanking him. “We’re so sorry, Anne.”

Anne listed. Joe slipped a firming arm around her shoulders and squeezed, surprised to feel her sink against him, letting him share the burden. She hadn’t done that before. Shoulders shaking, she stood silent, facing the coach.

“Thank you, Tom. Jeannine,” Joe answered when Anne stayed quiet. He nodded to the man who’d done so much for Anne. Tom Baldwin loved his protégés, those runners willing to go above and beyond. Anne. Jackie. Now, Missy. He was a man who put heart and soul into his job with a knack for seeing exceptional talent.

Sure, the guy was egocentric, a poster child for Springsteen’s *Glory Days*. Joe could never quite figure that out. At forty, Tom still flirted his way through a room, regardless of the occasion, even though he had a really nice wife and three cute kids. But you’d never know it when he was in a room full of women, regardless of age.

Feeling Anne shudder, Joe tightened his grip.

A brief stream of people walked by, offering condolences. By the time the line drew thin, Joe was glad it had been a small service. Anne had straightened after the first couple, but he’d kept his arm around her. Let people think what they would. He couldn’t stand by and watch her crumple out of spite.

His parents were the last to leave. Deb gathered Anne into a hug. “If you need anything, anything at all, you call,” she ordered lightly, stepping back, meeting Anne’s eye. “I mean it, Anne. You’re still family to us.”

Joe sent his mother an ‘oh, yeah?’ expression. She paid no attention. She stooped to shake Kyle’s hand. “My son tells me you know a lot about dinosaurs.”

Kyle's eyes widened. "Yes, ma'am. I know a lot of things."

"I bet you do." Deb McIntyre smiled at him. Straightening, she met Anne's eye once more. "Why don't you come home with us, dear? Have some lunch. We'd love to have you."

Anne faltered. "I couldn't. I..." She shrugged. Her eyes flitted to Joe then back to his mother. "I'm sorry. I can't."

Joe stiffened, but his mother didn't appear offended. "I understand. I'll come see you, Anne, if that's all right. Sometime soon?"

Anne nodded, relieved. "I'd like that."

"Good." Deb hugged her again, then stepped away to make room for Joe's father.

Jim's flat expression made it obvious he didn't share Deb's empathy. Joe cringed, realizing his father's antipathy reflected Joe's. His guilt magnified with Jim's gruff tone. "Sorry about your mother."

Anne nodded. "Thank you, sir."

Taking Deb's arm, the older McIntyre walked toward their car without another word. Anne glanced around, unsure. "It's over."

Joe nodded. "Yes. I'll take you home."

Staring at the nearly empty cemetery road, Anne frowned. "But, Sally—"

"I told her I'd see to you. Thought maybe you and Kyle would like a bite to eat."

She shifted her gaze to his. "That's nice of you, but we can't."

"I'm not my mother, Anne. I don't take no for an answer. You need to eat. So does Kyle. And he and I have dinosaurs to discuss."

He didn't want to fuel speculation by squiring her around, but the other option was to leave her alone after burying her mother. That made it no option. "Shall we say a prayer, first?" Inclining his head, he led her forward.

Anne prayed in silence, then lifted her head. The sheen of tears made her eyes shine like moonlit water, green, gold and gray. A man could drown in a pool like that.

Luckily, Joe was a great swimmer. He fought the urge to hold her, knowing his emotions were intensified by the feelings of the day. The fact that he was a caretaker and she needed help. Stepping back, he hoisted Kyle and turned to the car.

"Kyle gets to pick the restaurant," he decided, smiling at the same eyes he'd just turned from, set in a different face. Eyes he'd longed to reproduce with his pretty wife, had she stayed around long enough. Now someone else had beaten him to it.

The boy flung an arm around Joe's neck. The gesture made Joe hoist him higher. Tighter. He tried to dismiss the naturalness of the boy in his arms, the feel of Kyle's curls against his cheek, but he couldn't. He strode to the car, his emotions warring. Anger vied with caring, pride with humility.

Recognizing the internal struggle, Joe paused. Silencing a groan, he recalled Christ's teachings in the gospel of Luke. The story of the self-important Pharisee, lauding his goodness, his personal sacrifice, so haughty, so proud.

And the publican, a humble man, bowed before the Lord. It didn't take a whole lot of soul searching to figure out whom he resembled. Oh, he liked his standing with the town. Respect was an earned attribute, not to be taken lightly. A man in uniform should command deference for his integrity, his sense of fair play.

But pride held an evil lust. Narrowing his eyes, Joe glanced at Kyle. The boy's innocence drew him. Swallowing a sigh, Joe head-butted the child gently. "What do you want for lunch, Bud?"

Kyle didn't hesitate. "Nuggets."

Joe nodded, then dropped his gaze to Annie. "That okay with you?"

Her expression appeared worn but steadfast. "Fine."

Without thinking, Joe brushed his knuckles across her cheek, his graze gentle. "You're chilled. Hop in, we'll warm things up."

Anne's chin rose. Her lips parted, her eyes widened and her gaze searched his. He stepped back, swinging the door wide. Drawing a breath of cold, moist air, Joe watched as Kyle adjusted his belt. Once fastened, Joe moved around the back of the car, climbed into his seat and started the engine. The heater's blast chased the damp chill of the October day. He turned toward Anne. She met his gaze, her look questioning, her cheeks pink. From the cold or his touch? He wasn't sure, but he suspected the latter. Maybe hoped for the latter.

Shifting gears, Joe eyed the gravel road. It lay before him with no odd turns, a path that reflected Joe's life, his focus. He was in no mood for detours. Least of all, Anne Kellwyn's. His gaze aimed forward, Joe eased the car toward the predictability of a well-traveled lane holding no hidden curves.

CHAPTER TWELVE

The week crawled. Anne had more bereavement days, but went back to work on Friday. "I'm making myself crazy," she confessed to the principal "There's only so much cleaning a five room house can stand. It's better if I keep busy." Since the principal saw value in that for both of them, she agreed.

Working through the milling congregation at the close of Sunday service, Anne overheard a snip of conversation that slowed her steps.

"Triple bypass," offered an overweight woman. "And Tom so big on staying in shape. Why, you could have knocked me over with a feather when I heard that."

Thinking it would take a sizable feather, Anne bit back a smile.

"Jeannine is just overwrought," exclaimed the other woman.

Anne paused. Tom and Jeannine Baldwin were the only Tom and Jeannine she knew. Turning, she listened without remorse.

"He came through the surgery with no problems?" pressed the first woman, concerned.

"So they say. Jeannine's taking the kids up so they can see their dad's all right. I don't know who they'll get to coach the runners."

Placing a hand on one woman's arm, Anne asked, "Are you talking about Tom Baldwin?"

The heavy-set woman nodded. “Collapsed at the big meet in Rochester yesterday. They rushed him to Strong Memorial where he was operated on last night.”

The other woman eyed Anne. “He coached you, didn’t he?”

Anne nodded, wheels turning. With care, she masked her emotions. “How long will he be sick?” she asked, glancing from one to the other.

The first woman shrugged. “When my Harold had his bypass, he was out for six weeks. Tom’s younger, but,” she shrugged, “I would think at least that long.”

Anne nodded. “Thank you.”

Six weeks. That would put them into winter track. A man would be challenged to lead a young girl astray at fifteen below zero. Winter track training was primarily indoors, the strain of the frigid cold not good for lung capacity.

God granted her a reprieve. God and Tom Baldwin’s penchant for cheese fries and nachos. Now she needed to figure out what to do with the gift. What direction to take.

At least she had time to think things through. Kyle deserved more than being the innocent object of thoughtless action, just like that eighth grader deserved more than being the prey of a trusted predator.

Anne’s doorbell rang that evening. Joe stood on her porch, flanked by two official-looking men. Wondering, she opened the door.

The shorter man angled his head in question. “Ms. Kellwyn?”

Anne arched a brow to Joe. “You know who I am, Joe.”

He flushed, looking uncomfortable. “I’m on the Forest Hills School Board. This is an official visit.”

"Really?" She swung the door wider. "Come in."

She'd spent her days at home cleaning. The medical equipment was gone, leaving the room bigger. Airier. Joe glanced around, then caught her eye. "It feels different."

She nodded, silent. The absence of her mother was a dash of cold water every morning. A loss of laughter at night. Squaring her shoulders, she indicated for the men to sit. Two did.

Joe roamed.

The shorter man jumped right in, his voice agitated. "We have a question for you, Ms. Kellwyn."

Anne turned his way. "Yes?"

"As a running standout, you know how important our running program is to us, and can appreciate the opportunities Forest Hills has provided. College scholarships, awards, professional opportunities. The art and discipline of running trains both body and mind to overcome pain and obstacles in the quest for success."

He could have been reading from the Forest Hills student handbook. Probably memorized the paragraph on the way over. From the rotund look of him, Anne was pretty sure he'd never experienced the grill of distance running personally. She drew a breath, careful not to sigh. Or laugh.

The other man sent him a dubious look, then extended his hand to Anne. "James Johnson, Ms. Kellwyn. I'm the vice-president of the school board. Mr. Clemmons here," he indicated the other man with a shift of his chin, "is the current president. Chief McIntyre serves on the board as well."

Anne nodded, accepting his hand. "And you obviously know who I am. What puzzles me is why you're here? Has Kyle done something on the bus?"

Jim Johnson frowned, then smiled, relaxing. "No, of course not. I'm sorry, Ms. Kellwyn, perhaps we should start at the beginning. You know that Coach Baldwin suffered a heart attack yesterday?"

Anne kept her face composed. "I heard."

"He'll be out at least six weeks. Maybe more. We have a women's team that could be a contender at the state meet in Canandaigua next month. With our newest addition to the team, a strong finish is almost guaranteed as long as we don't lose more than one athlete to injury or illness."

"We need a coach," interjected Mr. Clemmons. "Someone to fill Tom's shoes. The position would be temporary, of course. Tom intends to resume his duties when he's able. In the meantime, we're in a pickle. With your running history, we were hoping you'd help us out."

Joe watched from across the room. Could he tell her mouth went dry, that her heart raced like an Amtrak express? She hoped not. Weighing the implications, she shook her head. "Gentlemen, I'm sorry, but—"

"Of course you'll be well compensated," Jim Johnson interrupted. Clemmons looked at him, his mouth agape. "Stepping into Tom Baldwin's shoes isn't easy, but if anyone could accomplish it, you could."

Maintaining a cool she didn't feel, Anne turned to him. "What makes you say that?"

"Your record in Toccoa was impressive," he stated mildly.

"You checked my records?" Anne bristled, straightening. "What gave you the right?"

The men exchanged looks. "We thought it prudent since we planned to offer you a position. We called your principal at Redmond, and—"

"You spoke with her as well?" Interrupting him, Anne leaned forward, amazed.

"Well, yes," offered Jim Johnson, confused by her reaction. "She speaks highly of you, and she assured me you maintained a sterling record down south."

"She did, huh?"

Anne stood. She tried to draw Joe into the conversation, but he kept his distance. Chin down, he studied something of great import on her worn hardwood floor. "Gentlemen, I hate to disappoint you, but I simply can't."

"But, surely," cut in Steve Clemmons, his look darting to Jim Johnson then back to her. "I know your days are full, Ms. Kellwyn..."

"With a five-year-old, a house, and a full-time job, yes. My days are full."

"We would have no problem with your son accompanying you. Invitationals, dual meets. Whatever it takes."

Anne's mind ran overtime.

She was a good coach. Her record in Toccoa proved that. She hadn't considered the possibility here, where anything to do with competitive running put her face to face with Tom Baldwin.

That couldn't happen. The twice she'd seen him already were too much. Coaching his team, using his office?

Impossible.

"Ms. Kellwyn?" Steve Clemmons' voice interrupted her thoughts.

"Hmm? Oh, yes, I'm sorry." The very idea of sitting in Tom's office, walking into that school...

No way. Standing, she shook her head. "I'm sorry, gentlemen. I know you're in a bind, but it's out of the question."

"Ms. Kellwyn, please. If you need time to consider?" Mr. Johnson stood as well, his expression pleading.

"I don't." Anne held her ground. "I'm quite certain. I'm sorry to disappoint you."

"We're only talking five weeks or so," Clemmons reminded her. "Surely five weeks isn't too much to ask for your alma mater? For a man who helped make you what you are? Educated, successful, self-assured."

Anne wanted to hit something. Or someone. Right now, Mr. Clemmons face was looking real good. She forced herself to step back. “Good day, gentlemen.”

Mr. Johnson acquiesced first. “Thank you for your time, Ms. Kellwyn.” He started for the door at an easy pace.

Mr. Clemmons seemed bewildered. In a school not big enough to host a football squad, cross-country and soccer were the big leagues on campus. To be on the team was a victory in itself. To coach the team, well...

In Forest Hills, successful high school coaches got dinners on the house, movie passes, free car washes. Oh, yeah, there were perks.

And with all that, Tom Baldwin wanted more. More than the money, prestige, respect and the freebies he was given.

He wanted their souls.

Well, he couldn’t have hers. She was stronger now, but there was no way she could set foot in Tom Baldwin’s office.

Joe hadn’t said a word. As the older men exited, he moved past her, chin down, eyes averted. Obviously he didn’t want her making too much out of his compassion at the funeral. She wouldn’t press, but she did want a chance to thank him for his kindness. When he reached the door, she put a hand on his forearm. “Joe.”

He turned. His normally bright blue eyes shadowed gray in disappointment.

The look coursed through her. The bitter note of disbelief in his voice sharpened the effect. “All the years Tom put into you, and you can’t give this little thing back? Five weeks to help kids have the chance you did. To be noticed. Maybe get a scholarship. After all Tom did for you.”

His resentment was palpable. He didn’t bother to shield the emotion. He stood rigid, his face stern. “Where would you be now if you hadn’t been one of

Tom's protégés? You think St. Lawrence University hefted you that money because of an eleven-ninety on your SATs?" He arched an indignant brow. "Think again, honey. That seventeen-twenty five-k did some serious talking.

"But that's right," he continued. "None of that matters. You couldn't wait to shake the dust off your feet when you left the first time, and I'm pretty sure you're not looking to get tied down here again. Does that about sum things up?"

He'd touched an amazing number of buttons for such a short speech. She wasn't sure which to disengage first, the mental, physical or emotional. All had jumped into high gear.

It didn't matter. There was no time to respond. Shaking his head, he went out the door, careful to pull it tight against the wind.

He didn't look back.

His reaction infuriated her. Deep, down, in-the-gut, you-have-no-idea-what-on-earth-you're-talking-about anger rose to choke her. What nerve he had, talking to her like that. As if she didn't care about the kids. Didn't want to help their cause.

She understood the pressure of being a top seed, a target for other runners to test their skills against. For some of these young athletes, this season could be it.

They'd done well at the McQuaid Invitational in Rochester, before their coach's collapse. Could she really turn her back on them, ignore their plight?

Are you tired of me yet, God? Sick of questions that have no answers?

Well, that makes two of us. One of us better figure out what's right and wrong here, because I'm way beyond confusion at this point. Beyond confusion and heading toward meltdown.

Help me before it gets that far, Lord. Don't send me into the jungle unprepared.

Joe's look had pierced her armor. He'd finally touched on the anger inside, and she saw how the resentment gnawed his spirit. Seeing that first-hand, she realized she should have contacted him. Written him. Done something so he didn't absorb a truckload of undeserved guilt over her disappearance.

Car lights flashed as Mary Ellen Fredericks returned Kyle from a play session. Opening the door, Anne let the peace of being his mother blanket her. Through all the mistakes, God had sent her a blessing. A reminder that life goes on.

Seeing Kyle's face, excited with the afternoon's activities, Joe's words haunted her. *"...to help kids who might have the chance you had."*

Kids like Kyle would be in ten years. Earnest, hard-working, respectful. Without giving herself time to rethink things, she grabbed the phone and punched in Joe's number. He answered swiftly, his voice gruff. "What?"

Caller I.D. She pulled a breath, wanting to respond in kind, then forced herself to rein in emotions that threatened to overrun her. "I changed my mind. I'll do it on one condition."

"And that is?" His tone was cold. Abrasive.

"Practices are in Redmond. Have them bus the kids over, I'll conduct the sessions from there or at the race sites. Not at Forest Hills."

"Of all the—"

"Take it or leave it."

Silence ensued, then Joe muttered, "I'll see to it."

Thank you, God. Anne nodded. "Thanks. Good night." She hung up before he could slam the receiver, then laughed at her foolishness.

Cell phones had nothing to slam. What satisfaction was there in that, she wondered, exclaiming over Kyle's newfound appreciation for anti-bacterial soap after a first-grade science lesson on germs. What did you do when you were angry with the person on the other end? Click them with your flash button?

Smiling at her inanity, she laid out a quick supper, glad her phone was the more old fashioned variety. There were times a girl needed to slam a receiver.

But not tonight. Not on Joe McIntyre.

CHAPTER 13

Anne assumed that coaching the high school team would be easy. She'd done it in Georgia. Piece of cake.

Uh, uh.

Clearing the practices with her principal hadn't posed a problem. She'd simply cited her need for proximity and the deal was done.

Dealing with a men's team that had been guided by Tom Baldwin? Another story.

They were guys. She was a woman. From the beginning they made it plain she had nothing to teach them.

The girls were receptive to her ideas, willing to go the distance. The guys ignored her and did their own thing.

By day three, she'd devised a plan. The men's team was not as strong as the women's competitively. Oh, sure, they ran faster. Testosterone, muscle mass, heart-lung capacity, slow-twitch muscle concentration. Put it all together and you had some nice performers, but nothing compared to their statewide counterparts. Obviously Tom hadn't spurred these boys to press beyond the pain in their quest for excellence.

Anne knew there was no alternative to hard work.

These boys didn't believe it. They were strong enough to win their sectional title, but they'd be eaten alive in Canandaigua. Puffing their chests like young roosters, they preened as if they were all new editions of Steve Prefontaine. Please.

The girls were ambitious, dedicated to Tom and the cause. Searching their eyes, she felt confident that none of them had been victimized, including the thirteen-year-old wonder child, Missy Volmer.

When the boys returned from their supposed five-mile run, Anne stood waiting. Unless they'd all sprouted wings, there was no way they finished a five-mile loop in twenty-one minutes. Grinning, she met them at the back door. "Ready?"

They eyed her. "For?" one asked, hip cocked, his tone insolent.

"Stage two," she announced. Leaving the assistant to wait for the girls' team, she headed downhill. "Let's go, men."

They exchanged looks of disgust, then followed her half-heartedly. By the time they'd stroked off the first mile, they alternated trying to break her lead.

She matched them, stride for stride, no matter how much it hurt, and by mile three, oh, yeah. She was hurting.

But she'd die before she let it show.

Bounding up hills, through narrow paths that led into woods, she maintained a five-forty pace that wore them down.

A couple dropped back. Way back.

Anne kept running.

A wiry senior challenged her lead through town. Obviously the notion of running behind a woman through populated areas didn't sit well.

Anne held him off, nodding to the passers-by as she careened through the streets before heading back to the school. In an area where running well meant so much, these boys just flunked the test.

Back at the gym, she waited, walking off the lactic acid, seeing the girls eye her with newfound respect.

The boys straggled in, looking beat. She glanced up, her expression even. "Grab a shower, get changed, and meet me in the gym."

Grumbled responses met her command. She turned a deaf ear to the rumble. Missy Volmer sidled up, eyes wide. "You still run like that?"

Anne nodded. "Every day I can."

"But you don't compete."

Anne shrugged. "I hop into some road races. Bring home a few prizes. Nothing big league."

"Why?"

Anne faced the youngster she swore to protect, someway, somehow. "Running was good for me. Competing taught me self-discipline, self-control. How to set goals and work toward them. But being a runner wasn't the be-all, so many make it out to be. I wanted balance," she finished with a shrug. "I'd achieved my education, a lot of first-place medals and trophies." Smiling, she admitted, "And a lot of second-place trophies as well. I learned that being second doesn't have to mean you're the first loser."

Missy stared at Anne, her expression bright. "You're still good."

Anne winked. "Oh, yeah. But, more importantly?" Missy arched her brows, waiting. "I'm a good teacher and a great mom. Running's moved down the list." She watched as the youngster absorbed the message, then turned as discontented noises approached the south door.

The boys filtered in, distraught. She motioned them to sit. Some did, some ignored her. In turn, she ignored that.

"Right now you're mad." She addressed them en masse, eyeing the group. "You're thinking: 'What's she doing, dragging us out after a grueling five miler just to show us up through the streets of one of the toughest running areas in the state.' Right?"

If looks could kill, she'd have been buying a coffin. She met those looks head on. "Let me give it to you straight. You're slackers."

They gaped.

She nodded, tapping a toe against a riser. "You know it and I know it. You figure there's nothing you can learn from a woman, nothing you need to learn from a woman and nothing you want to learn from a woman. That sum things up?"

"In a nutshell."

She wasn't sure which one commented, but it didn't matter. She nodded, working her jaw. "I thought as much. Well, here's the deal. If you're content to be big fish in a small pool, that's fine. You can wrap up a win in your section, tout your abilities around town and end up paying the full shot at a state university. Or pump gas." She gave that a minute to sink in. A couple of boys squirmed. "Or you can get your heads out of the sand and work to compete at a more significant level. You think the times you're showing are good?"

A few more fidgeted as she handed out current standings of Class D teams. "Feast your eyes, gentlemen. Check the numbers. Where do you fit? Try page two."

At their crestfallen looks, she changed her tune. "You're not a bad bunch. You got dealt a rough blow because your coach got sick and you've got a know-it-all woman saying you stink."

Chins jerked up. Smooth, she continued, "No one said this was going to be easy. You've got five weeks before states. That isn't long, but it could be enough to come out of this with times that garner some notice. Especially you juniors with your senior year to look forward to." She struck a chord. A few eyes sparked with interest. Anne contemplated the group, keeping her voice straightforward.

"You can either sit around, feeling sorry for yourselves, or you can work the way you should have been working all along. Unload your Neanderthalic notions about women and come to practice ready to train. You think I showed you up today, running fresh and rested after you ran your initial loop, right?"

Several nodded. A tall, gangly senior spoke up. "That's what you did, right?"

"Wrong." She held out her sports watch. "There's my time for my initial five. A five *I didn't* cut corners on." She paused, watching, waiting for the truth to sink in. "I ran it before the bus brought you in."

Eyes widened in respect. Some in disbelief. "Ran it right through town, boys." She addressed the skeptics with a lift of her brow. "Check with the locals if you don't believe me. There are two things you can count on." Standing tall, she met them eye-to-eye. "I'm honest and I'm fast. Real fast. If you want to improve these times," she tapped the paper in her hand, "then listen to your coach. I'll see you tomorrow."

They straggled out. The girls looked as though they'd found a champion for their cause. A movement at the door caused Anne to turn.

Joe walked in, looking too good to be believed. What was it about a man in navy wool? The cut of the uniform showcased his broad shoulders, narrow waist. She bit back a sigh as he walked her way. Removing his cap, he faced her. "Things okay?"

Still gruff, but not angry. A marked improvement. She nodded.

Missy spouted, "Things are great. Coach Kellwyn beat the boys in a run through town. I guess that showed them!" She said it with the heightened enthusiasm of an adolescent girl.

Joe struggled not to smile. "The boys giving you a hard time?"

"I think we've got a handle on it," she replied. She looked toward the girls and jerked her head toward the lockers. "I'll see you tomorrow."

It was obvious that some would rather watch the adult interplay, but they left. Just somewhat slowly. Joe twisted his hat. "I wanted to stop by and thank you. I over-reacted the other night." He paused, his brow furrowed, choosing his words. "I didn't mean to come down so hard on you."

"Joe." Biting her lip she looked away, then disciplined herself to bring her eyes back to his. "I hurt you. I'm only now beginning to understand how much. How my disappearance and silence made things for you. If I could go back? Change things?"

He stepped forward, his eyes curious. Almost eager. "What would you change, Annie? What could I have done different?"

"Oh, Joe." Tears welled at the tone in his voice. "It was never you. You were wonderful. So good. It was me. I was the one lacking. But I didn't know how to fix things, so I ran away. Made more mistakes."

"Kyle."

She stared at a spot on the whitewashed wall. "His father was a mistake." She dropped her gaze to her shoes for long seconds, her hands tingling with the words to come. "Only one of many, Joe." She didn't dare look up to see how those words affected him. She really didn't want to know. "The boy is a blessing."

"He's here," Joe offered, shrugging one shoulder toward the door. His voice was matter-of-fact, not condemning. She wasn't sure what to make of that. "He was making clay figures with the art teacher a few minutes ago. Sally's mother had a spell in the nursing home, so she needed someone to take charge of Kyle. She called me."

"She did?" Anne looked up, surprised.

"Yeah. I hope that was okay. We talked dinosaurs and stuff. Then I figured he might want to see where you work."

"Joe."

"I owed you an apology, Anne. I shouldn't have railed on you that way. It's just..."

"I bring out the worst in you without even trying?" she quipped, trying to lighten the moment as she moved toward the door.

He grimaced. "Or the best, depending on the day."

She sharpened her look at his response. "I don't think that's much of a factor anymore."

Kyle raced in, waving a five-year-old's rendition of a diplodocus in Plasticine. Anne smiled, grateful for the change in subject.

Joe palmed the boy's head. Leaning back, Kyle grinned up at him. "My tooth is very loose," he informed Joe, wiggling it with his tongue. "When it comes out, the tooth fairy will bring me money."

"Really?" Joe looked at him with interest. "My teeth are bigger. If mine fall out, do I get more money?"

Kyle shrugged. "Probly."

"Probably," corrected Anne, emphasizing the second syllable. "And I like Joe with his teeth."

"Do you, Anne?"

The note in his voice sent a shiver of hope down her spine. She didn't look up. "Yes."

There was an awkward silence. Anne broke the quiet, moving to the door, her hand out to Kyle. "All right, big fella, we've got to get you home. You've got reading to do and I've got supper to make."

"There's always Burger King," Joe offered.

Anne's eyes shot to his. He watched her with a half-hooded expression, making it impossible to read his meaning.

"I've got spaghetti sauce thawed at home," she told him, unsure what else to say. On a whim, she added, "Would you like to have pasta with us?"

For a moment his eyes lit, then he leveled the look and shook his head. "Another time, maybe. I'm on duty 'til seven."

"We can eat late," Kyle interjected. "I could help my mom, then do homework, and Joe could still have supper with us."

Everything appeared easy in the eyes of a child. So deceptively simple. Joe stepped forward, then back. "Not tonight, Bud." At Kyle's look of disappointment, Joe offered, "Did I hear you have a birthday coming up?"

Kyle nodded. It hadn't been the happiest of subjects. A birthday party so soon after losing Maura seemed disrespectful. Still, he was a little boy about to turn six. Joe turned to Anne. "Can we do Burger King on Saturday, after the race? Have a bunch of his friends from school and do a little party there?" Somehow he must have known a traditional party would be tough on her.

She nodded. "That's a great idea."

"Really, Mom?" Kyle's eyes lit with glee. "Bobby Osborne had a birthday party at Burger King once. He said it was awesome."

"Oh, yeah?" She smiled down at him as they moved through the door. Reaching out, Joe pushed the door wider. His hand grazed the side of her face, fluttered her hair. She paused at the touch, looking straight ahead.

Memories swept her. Joe's touch, his smile. The way he looked at her as if she were the sweetest thing. Why couldn't that have been the case?

Kyle looked back. "Mom? You coming?"

She didn't realize she'd stopped. So had Joe, his arm outstretched, her face against his sleeve. Startled, she stepped ahead, then glanced back.

He studied her with such a look of confusion that she wanted to smooth his brow. Instead, she quick-stepped down the hall until Kyle had to half-run to keep up. Grabbing her planning book, she turned, a mustered smile on her face. "Thanks, Joe. For everything."

He sported that hooded look again, the one that protected him from dragons, velociraptors, villains and ex-wives. "No problem. What time shall we plan for Saturday? Three o'clock?"

Her jaw dropped. She saw his eyes note that. His head tilted as he glanced to her mouth. "You're coming?" It took all her concentration to form the words, then say them out loud.

"I thought that was the plan." Reaching out, he tapped her chin up, closing her mouth. "That give you enough time to get back from the race, get cleaned up?"

She considered the time frame. "Better make it four."

He nodded. "Four it is. You invite the kids. I'll take care of the rest."

"Joe."

Quiet, he strode to the door, looking just as good from behind as he did from the front. He waved a hand of dismissal into the air. "Saturday."

CHAPTER 14

Anne glared at her watch as the bus lumbered into the lot. Of all days for the driver to be late picking up the team, this was the worst. Her watch read four-oh-five, the guests would be waiting for Kyle, and she looked like she'd spent eight hours outside in the damp chill of a brisk October day because she had.

She smelled like moldy leaves and gym shorts, her hair was pulled back and banded under the ski cap that had become a necessity due to an icy northwest wind...

Why had she said yes to this, never factoring her appearance? As she exited the bus, the driver cast her another look of apology. "Coach, I really am sorry."

He'd gotten lost in the city, back-tracked, then ended up south of them in the convoluted park. It had taken nearly an extra hour for him to find the proper spot. By then the team was cold, disheartened, hungry and whiny.

So was Kyle.

With forgiveness she wasn't sure she felt, Anne patted the driver's shoulder. "It builds character, Red. No big deal. We all survived."

He smiled in gratitude. "Tom wouldn't have been so forgiving."

Anne shrugged. "Everyone's different."

By the time she found a parking spot at the restaurant, it was four-eighteen. Kyle stopped whining now that the actual moment of the party had come. His eyes shone in the thinning light.

She bustled him in, making apology. Joe took one look and gave her a heart-stopping grin. "You look—"

"Don't," she snapped, feeling wretched. "It's a little kids' party and my looks don't factor in."

"Great," he finished.

"What?"

"What what?"

"You said great. Did you mean—?"

"Yes."

"I'm a mess."

His grin widened. "Yes, again."

"My hair." She cast a rueful glance upward. "I had to wear a hat all day, and it rained and everything smells like rotting leaves."

Joe sniffed, smiled and shook his head. "Not everything." Turning then, he led Kyle to the noisy crew in the back corner.

Gulping, Anne followed.

They had a ball. The kids laughed, ate, and offered Kyle presents that made his eyes huge.

By the end everyone was happy and Anne forgot about her seedy appearance until she washed her hands in the ladies' room.

The mirror brought everything into perspective. She groaned at the first glimpse, then laughed. The difference of motherhood, she mused, wiping her hands. Right now, what truly mattered was that Kyle had a good day. Something fun to remember.

Walking through the filling restaurant, she saw Joe tuck his wallet away as the counter girl slid bills into her apron, her expression grateful. "You tipped her."

He nodded as he watched three boys arm wrestle.

"I could have done that."

Joe shifted his gaze to her. "I wanted to take care of this. Kyle's a good kid."

"You paid the bill?"

"Yes."

"Joe, you can't-"

"Already did."

"But-"

He stepped forward, ignoring her protest, coaching the boys in the finer points of arm wrestling. Shaking her head, she cleaned up the ice cream cups and straw wrappers, watching him with Kyle.

How easy it would be for the boy to fall in love with the broad-shouldered man beside him. Joe was meant to settle down, have children. Had she spoiled that for him? Did he hate women so much that he'd never trust again?

And who would he pick, she mused, smiling as he challenged a first-grader, making mock looks of exaggerated pain while his arm caved to the tabletop.

Jenna somebody-or-other? The one who didn't understand his penchant for nature? Who'd probably never stood in a creek wearing ugly rubber waders, casting a line she'd baited herself while he stood close, his smile proud.

Had Jenna ever prowled the woods at his side, learning the aspects of hunting, seeing the care Joe took no matter what he did? Or had he cooked her venison stew, seasoned just right, loaded with carrots and potatoes, mushrooms and onions?

One forkful would be inducement enough. Joe was the quintessential outdoorsman. The hunter/gatherer, working to provide for his family. Silly, silly girl.

He turned then. Met her eye. Something in her expression sharpened his gaze. His left eye narrowed. A muscle in his cheek twitched. He studied her a moment, then turned back.

By the time everyone picked up their sons, it was nearly six-fifteen.

"This was fun," crowed Kyle, helping Joe tote presents to the car. "Thanks, Mom. Thanks, Joe."

Joe's amused eyes met hers. "You're welcome, Bud. What do you say we get your mommy home so she can clean up?"

"Grr..." She sent Joe a mock frown. "I'd almost managed to forget how bad I look. Thanks for the reminder."

"Glad to oblige. Kyle, you want to ride with me?"

"In the police car?" Kyle's eyes went round. He turned to Anne. "Can I? Please?"

"You don't mind?" Anne looked up at Joe. He shook his head and tousled the boy's hair.

"Naw. It's practically on the way. Come on, Bud."

Kyle and Joe unloaded the gifts at Anne's. Stepping into the house, a chill air swept them. Joe frowned. "The heat not working?"

Anne shrugged. "I didn't want to run it all day while we were gone. I figured I'd start a fire tonight."

"Frugal." He looked at her, considering. "I'll see to the fire. You go shower." Crossing the room, he adjusted the thermostat, satisfied when the furnace rumbled to life below them. "I'll turn this on long enough to take the chill off."

"Make yourself at home, Joe."

He turned and smiled at the expression on her face. "Glad to."

"It's not like it's freezing in here."

He huffed a breath, looking for vapor. "Almost."

He headed to the wood stove. "No kindling?"

"Sure there is. I chopped it in my spare time."

He bit back a smile. "I'll drop some off. You shouldn't need much. Once the cold hits, it's better to keep a constant bed of coals to restart the fire." He noted her expression. "You know how to bank a fire, right?" When she pressed her lips together, he sighed. "I'll show you. It's not hard, it's just a... technique. Can you start a fire, Anne? Get one going?"

"Most of the time."

"Shame on you. A North Country girl who can't make fire? Your prehistoric ancestors would be disgraced." As he chastised, he gathered an armload of wood. He eyed the logs in disgust. "Where'd you get this?"

"I ordered wood from Dale Edwardson. Is it all right?"

Joe scowled. "It's soft maple and green to boot." He handed her a piece. "Feel how light that is? Hard wood's heavy. Dense. Whole different texture and smell."

Anne bit her lip. "I should have realized that, huh?"

His tone softened. "Not necessarily. Most people think a log's a log. Kyle, can you get me some old newspapers?"

"Sure."

Without a word of argument, the boy complied. Obviously making fire ranked above cleaning up toys. Anne puckered her brow at the maleness of it all. "I didn't have a stove down south. And Dad always took care of ours. Then Mom took over."

"You need to learn." It was Joe's take-charge voice now. "If the furnace broke down or the electricity went off, how would you keep warm?"

"Call my landlord?"

His eyes swept up. Met hers. Something flashed in that look, that connection. Her heart danced a jig in her chest. Joe angled his head, watching her as Kyle returned. Accepting the papers, his gaze stayed locked with Anne's. His eyes warmed her, his look steadfast. Then he worked his jaw, jerked a shoulder and glanced down at Kyle, breaking the connection.

Chill coursed through her without his look, the warmth in his eyes. Backing up, she headed into the bathroom after grabbing fresh clothes. When she returned, washed and renewed, Joe stood, ready to bolt. A merry fire danced in the stove, the house cozy with the combined attentions of Joe and the furnace.

"You're set then?"

She noted Kyle playing on the floor, surrounded by new toys. "Yes. Thank you."

"Hey, Bud. Happy Birthday."

Kyle scrambled to his feet. "Thanks, Joe. And thanks for the dinosaur." He handed his new treasure to Anne. "It's really neat."

"Wow." Anne examined the carved wooden figure. "That's magnificent. Did Hi do this?"

Joe nodded.

"It's wonderful." Grateful, she met his gaze. "Thank you. For everything."

"Gotta go." He turned, moving to the door.

"Of course." Planting her polite smile into place, Anne followed. What had she expected? That Joe could overlook the years of pain she'd caused? Brush away her sinfulness, her immorality? Not likely.

Joe did an about face at the entry, his look stern.

"Fill the wood box before you go to bed. Open the bottom draft, let it catch. Give it a couple of minutes. Then, shut the drafts down. All of them. You should still have a bed of coals in the morning."

"Fill it, open it, torque it, shut it. Got it."

He didn't smile. He looked anxious. Bothered. "All right. Good night."

Gone was the humorous, gentle man who'd played with a band of rowdy six-year-olds. Anne bit back disappointment. It was too nice an evening to ruin with grown-up feelings. She nodded, keeping her face serene. "Good night, Joe."

Joe climbed into the SUV, heart racing, palms sweaty.

It felt good. Too good. Sitting there, playing with the boy, hearing the sounds of Anne's shower, knowing she'd rejoin them, fresh and clean. As if he belonged there, tending the fire, gathering wood, eating cookies from the old ceramic jar her mother used.

He'd choked, almost literally.

What was he thinking? Why would he even consider the possibility? He wasn't desperate or needy. Life was good, all in all. Strong, steady. What he absolutely, positively did not need was the basketful of baggage that came with Anne Louise Kellwyn.

How foolish would he appear? Taking up with her would be non-surgical emasculation. How would anyone respect him after what she'd done?

No, better to see this for what it was. An old attraction, unresolved. Perfectly understandable. Forget that he'd transported ten years back in time when she'd walked into the restaurant looking like a drowned rat. How many times had he seen her like that at the end of a day's racing? Too many to count.

And she'd always been beautiful to him. Her splendor was more than appearance, though he saw nothing wrong with Anne's looks. The straight brow, no hint of a widow's peak. Round, wide eyes, sometimes guarded, often expressive. Her mouth, soft and full, ready to spring into a quick smile or a tempting kiss.

Except for those last weeks of their marriage. Then she hadn't smiled at all. Tears slipped down her cheeks for no reason she would share. How often had he held her, promising everything would be all right?

Constantly. Her sadness scared him. Bewildered him. He had no clue as to the cause. Was it him? Did she regret marrying him? How could she when everything between them was so perfect, so beautiful, their life together so fulfilling?

He'd come home one day, full of questions that needed answers, ready to haul her to the doctor. He had to know what triggered the lapse into depression for his pretty, talented wife.

Open closets greeted him. Empty drawers.

She'd cleaned out, leaving nothing but a terse note and a teal-toned sweater he found behind the couch two months later.

He cried when he found that sweater, remembering how it softened her eyes to gray-green. How the cowl neck slouched against her shoulders, the fan of walnut hair thick against the knit.

"I can't do this, God," he prayed, heading up his drive. "Not a second time. I loved her once and it nearly killed me. I can't do it again. I won't do it again."

Parking the cruiser, he stepped into the cold, clear night. Stars shone as they never could near a city. Bright and luminous, they sparked in the crystal air of the northern latitude. "I don't want to hurt her, Lord, but I can't see her, either. When I'm with her..." He closed his eyes, thinking. "I'm not sure where I am. Who I am. If what I'm feeling is old stuff, rehashed, or something else.

"I want her." It felt weird, admitting that to God. "She's drawn me from the time I belted Richie Wilkes for calling her an alien. But she might as well be an alien, because I don't understand her. And I can't trust her. Love isn't love without trust."

He sighed, puzzling his emotions. Attraction? Lust? He frowned, knowing his feelings for Anne went beyond physical desire. Something in her called to him. Was she his Siren, his lure? His temptation into stupidity?

Well, he'd been a fisherman a long time. He knew the best spots, all the right moves. Even so, you didn't always catch what you were angling for. Sometimes the hook held a surprise.

Joe didn't need a surprise. If this was a case of 'fish or cut bait', he'd clip his line. No way would he become a laughingstock by taking up with the woman who'd humiliated him already.

So what that she was the most beautiful, winsome thing he'd ever laid eyes on, even after a day of running the woods, mud splatters dotting the backs of her legs, her hair mashed from a knit cap pulled snug to warm her ears.

He wasn't a bit interested.

He sighed. Yeah. Right.

CHAPTER 15

"I saw your Mrs. the other day." Boog Camden applied some kind of gold-tinged stain to another rocker a few weeks later, the striped grain springing to life beneath the work of his hands. Joe had spent those weeks avoiding Anne and the boy in any way, shape or form. He'd given due diligence to staying off Old Orchard Road.

It hadn't helped. Because even though he hadn't seen her, he couldn't stop thinking about her and that alone was driving him crazy.

"Buying a turkey breast," Boog went on. "For the holiday next week, I suspect."

"She's not my missus anymore." Joe's voice held a note of warning. He clenched his coffee cup tighter, remembering how it felt to find Anne's name on the Florida State registry. At that moment he'd realized the truth in Maura's words. Anne had chosen a different path, plain and simple. One that didn't include him.

"Pieces of paper don't mean so much," Boog mused. "What's in the heart, what God intended? That's where there's meaning, Chief."

Joe arced a brow. "Adding philosopher and theologian to your résumé, Boog? That's a lot of hats to wear."

Boog concentrated on rubbing the stain into the oak's grain, then raised knowing eyes. "Just common sense."

Joe met the gaze with his own steady look. "There are times when it's better to mind your own business. How's my chair?"

Boog let the first comment go. "Almost done. Just needs staining and finishing. It's in the back room if you care to look."

"I'll wait 'til it's ready." He ran a blunt finger along the curve of the etched oak back. "This is a beautiful piece. I think it's even prettier in the oak. An order?"

"Of a sort. I get calls for these at Christmas." The craftsman eyed the ivy and briar rose design pressed into the headrest of the rocker. "It's a piece that says home. Family."

Joe agreed. The golden oak chair represented home fires burning. Cozy suppers. A baby suckling at a life-giving breast, hands clenched, curled against its mother's warmth. Straightening, he took a long drag on his coffee cup. "Gotta go. Thanks for the coffee."

Boog nodded, affable. "Anytime, Chief."

A turkey breast, huh?

The notion gnawed at Joe, just what Boog intended, he was sure. All his talk about mothers and rockers, holidays and turkey breasts.

Who'd have expected his friend to be the town romantic? Not Joe. Boog, with his singular ways, his silent past, his uncanny knack for sizing a situation. The whole thing was funny in a Mayberry sort of way. Or it would be if Joe weren't the object of Boog's attention.

But, a turkey breast? That's not Thanksgiving, Joe mused. *You can't make decent gravy without dark meat juices, and a turkey breast is all white.* Stopping by

Abe's grocery, he questioned the old man. "Abe, have you ever made decent gravy from a turkey breast?"

Always quick to spot a sale, Abe nodded. "They put a packet of seasoning stuff in there so you can make it up quick. Way easier than the real thing."

Joe groaned inside. A turkey breast with pretend gravy. For Thanksgiving. Wrong in more ways than a country boy like him could count.

He'd followed the progress of the running teams. He'd even stopped in at a meet the week before. Anne's teams had done well, the girls placing first against all four schools and the boys doing the same against three of the four.

The guys' times had improved. They could place in the state meet if they got lucky.

They didn't. It was close, but Section Five sent strong competition, and they nudged Forest Hills back two places. Better than they would have done, Joe mused, noting the improvement in their times. But not quite good enough.

The girls placed second at states. First went to a downstate school, but the girls' team from Forest Hills wasn't disheartened. All but one would return next year, with Missy more experienced. They had high hopes and dreams.

That meant Annie's coaching was done, Joe thought on the afternoon before Thanksgiving. Tom should be back in two weeks, and winter track didn't start until mid-December.

He deliberately hadn't seen Annie since Kyle's party. He'd avoided her at the cross-country meet. The air held too much raw emotion, and he felt no need to tempt fate. Once burned, twice careful. Conversely, her growing acceptance from some townsfolk created its own problems. Short weeks previous, before her successful coaching stint, people spoke her name in hushed asides, their looks commiserative. Now it was

Anne-this and Annie-that, tossing references out as if she hadn't cast him aside like a pair of well-trod Nikes.

Did he want her punished? Ostracized? Yes and no. That realization shamed him.

He visited the local hospice before heading home. Both beds were occupied, and he knew the volunteers might have a rough time. Death and holidays made a bitter mix.

Kathy Partridge greeted him. "Joe. How are you? Having Thanksgiving at your parents'?"

He nodded, removing his hat. "Yes. You doing it at home or going out?"

She slid a glance left. "Probably right here. Alva's slipping."

"Ah." Volunteers stayed throughout the last hours, preferring not to break ranks with a change of shift. "And Hank?"

"He'll be eating turkey with the family." She chuckled. "I told him there might be some mistake. A man at death's door should not be so cheerful. So full of life."

Joe laughed. "And he said?"

"That eternal life waits and he welcomes it gladly," she quoted. "He's quite a man."

"Always was." Joe stepped in further, laying his hat aside. "I wanted to visit before heading home."

"Good of you, Chief. Would you like some pie before you see them? We have pecan and apple. Homemade."

"Really?" He loved pecan pie. "A slice of pecan would hit the spot. I don't think supper's a reality tonight." It was already seven-ten and he felt bone-weary, in no mood to cook.

She brought the slice to him with a little fork. "A dessert fork," she told him, pointing out the size. "Pie never tastes as good on a long fork."

He wasn't sure that was true, but the pie was melt-in-your-mouth wonderful. "Whoever made this knew what they were doing. Best pecan pie I've ever had."

"Joe, how funny." Kathy shot him an amused look. "Your Annie made it. Brought them by a little while ago. Said she loved to bake and it seemed funny to heat up the oven for just her and the boy. I guess she used to bake for a church kitchen down south. It sure is good, don't you think?"

Better than good, but his words heard one phrase only. *Your Annie.*

She wasn't his anything. Not his Annie, his girl, his wife, his lover, the mother of his children...

He took a breath. It would do no good to correct Kathy. She said what came naturally. When two people go around together, then marry, it's hard to picture them apart.

Unless they've spent eight years apart. Then it should be tricky to picture them together. Or downright impossible.

But the pie was wonderful. He'd have to compliment Anne on that. At least the enforced hiatus had improved her cooking skills. Quiet, he handed the empty plate to Kathy. "Thank you. I'll see Hank first."

"He'll appreciate that, Chief. The families, too. They love that you care."

He knew that. He understood that was why so many had reacted negatively to Annie's reappearance. Joe took care of the community. They reciprocated. Things were like that in Forest Hills. Solid and good. Until the self-righteous banded together to keep out the sinners, the prodigals. Then good lent itself to evil.

Driving to his mother's, he prayed for guidance. He'd quashed the complaints of some, letting them know Annie wasn't fair game. Her coaching had coaxed others to her favor. That she was willing to help out meant a lot to some locals.

But there were still those who wagged their tongues. Joe grimaced. He might be one of them if he weren't a featured player.

Opening his parents' front door, the aroma of pumpkin mixed with the essence of sage. Preparations for the holiday were well under way. His mother's family always came up from Ogdensburg, toting cakes and puddings. The dessert bar at a McIntyre holiday dinner was something to behold, laden and good. He followed his nose to the over-sized kitchen where his mother bustled.

"Joe." She laughed and gave him a hug. "Just in time. Greg's been called out and I need someone to test this stuffing, make sure it's right. You were always the best stuffing taster."

"My pleasure, Ma'am." He doffed his cap in respect. "Just show me the bowl."

No bowl, but he knew that. Deb McIntyre kept an over-sized dishpan for such things. His mother may have had only two children, but years of running a hunting lodge taught her to cook for an army.

"Behind you." Deb McIntyre waved a pushing dowel in his direction.

"You're grinding cranberries?"

"Yup."

"That's my favorite job." He'd ground the berries and oranges for his mother's homemade relish for as long as he could remember.

"Be my guest." Stepping aside, she eyed his uniform. "You might want to change, first. They spatter."

"Good point. Stop grinding."

Grinning, she moved to a large pile of sweet potatoes. "Not to worry. There's plenty to do."

"Where's Dad?"

She rolled her eyes. "Napping. Hunting wore him out. He needed to rest before he turns in for the night."

Joe grinned at her dour expression. "I'd have been with him if I hadn't been working. Great day for walking the woods."

"Yeah, yeah, yeah." She waved him off. "I've heard it all before. Get some grub clothes on. There's stuff in your old room. Don't be messing up that expensive wool."

The Kitchen-Aide grinder stood waiting when he returned. "Are the oranges in the fridge?"

Deb nodded. "Right hand side. How was your day?"

He shrugged. "All right. Fairly calm except for people picking up their kids."

"Money in the bank," she noted, smiling. The number of people tapped for speeding on college influx weekends rose markedly. "New uniforms, all around!"

Joe laughed. "By the end of freshman year the parents figure out that the posted speed limits mean what they say. The students?" He shook his head. "They take longer."

"Joe, can you move those pies to the buffet?" His mother nodded beyond him. "I need more room and they're cool enough now."

"Sure thing." Toting the apple and cherry deep-dish offerings, he paused at the door. "You ever think of making pecan pie for Thanksgiving?"

Deb turned. "I didn't, no. I wish you'd asked me earlier. I love pecan pie."

Joe nodded. "So do I."

When he swung back through the door, his mother asked, "What's Annie doing tomorrow?"

He managed an instant leap to the defensive like a great soccer move from back in the day. "I have no idea."

"Oh." She dropped thick-sliced sweet potatoes into a large kettle. *Plunk. Plunk. Plunk.*

Joe started the grinder, then paused it. "Why do you ask?"

She didn't look up. "Just curious."

"Mm hmm." For a second time, Joe hit the power button. He ground an orange, peel and all, then stopped the machine once more. "You always have a reason, Mom."

"Generally."

"We are not inviting Annie and the kid over here for Thanksgiving, if that's what you're getting at."

Deb turned, surprised. "Did I say that?"

"No, but you're thinking it." Heat built under Joe's collar as he flipped the switch forward. A half-bag of cranberries met the blade before he stopped this time. "How awkward do you think that would be? Anne sitting there with the boy, the family gathered around, wondering where he came from, wondering why she was here, wondering..."

His voice rose. Trying to contain himself, he turned back to the fruit, hit the switch, and ground another orange into oblivion. Then more berries. He didn't know why he alternated since he'd mix them once done, but he'd always done it this way and saw no reason to change now. Scowling, he ground the last orange before hitting the power button one final time.

The silence left a void. As he poured the sugar, he muttered, then turned, waving a spoon, his voice incredulous. "Why would you even bring that up?"

Deb turned calm eyes his way. "Because she just buried her mother, she's alone, most of the town has snubbed her and I like her." She shifted one shoulder slightly. "Simple enough. Unless your pride means more than human suffering."

"My pride?" Deliberate, Joe put down the mixing spoon rather than throw it. "What pride? Any pride I had got flushed when she walked out, letting the world know I wasn't good enough for her. Who's got pride after that?"

"You, from the sound of it."

He strode across the room, banged through the swinging door, then came back, seconds later. "I don't understand," he spouted, struggling to stay reasonable. "I'm your son. Have been for nearly thirty-five years. She was my wife for half a year, more or less. You're willing to sacrifice my feelings to be nice to her? What are you thinking?" He was whining and knew it. He didn't care.

Deb faced him. "First, watch your tone of voice. I'm still your mother. Second, whatever happened in that marriage is between the two of you. Obviously you still haven't talked it through, and neither one of you will find peace until you do. Third, I wouldn't sacrifice you to anything, Joe. I don't have the strength of Abraham. But you keep looking at this whole thing from your vantage point. What happened to you, how you felt. What Anne did to *you*."

She shook her head, concerned. "Who took care of Anne? A woman who logged a thousand miles to run from whatever hurt her. Annie Kellwyn, the wonder child we loved, who acted out of character to escape something. Or someone. Who took care of Annie, Joe? All these years that people gathered around you, showing you their support, who did Anne have? I'll tell you." The look on her face made it plain she'd do just that.

Wonderful.

"No one," she continued, brandishing a sweet potato. "Her father dead, her mother unable to travel. She made a life for herself with no help. You've seen your friends, what it was like for them to have children." Concern deepened Deb's voice. "Sleepless nights, crazy days. Anne finished her education, had a child, raised that child and worked all the while. I couldn't have done it."

"Wouldn't have done it," Joe corrected. "You wouldn't have chucked Dad and slept around. We're talking two different people."

"Are things that simple?" Deb challenged. "You can write this off as her mistake, her problem?"

That stung. Hadn't he tortured himself over what he could have done different? Prayed? Begged? There was nothing. No answer at all.

He hadn't blamed God. Not on your life. He just figured Annie was a puzzle to the Lord, Himself and left it at that.

"You never went after her." His mother's voice stayed calm. "Why?"

"She didn't want me." In return he kept his voice unyielding. "She'd started a new life, on her own. I wasn't about to chase her."

"Exactly."

They'd come back to pride. He knew it. She knew it.

"Joe." Deb moved forward, putting her arms around her son. "I love you. But you've suffered with this; she's suffered with this. It's time to get things out in the open, move on."

He stepped away from her embrace. "I moved on a long time ago," he retorted. "You're the one still clinging to some kind of pie-in-the-sky hope." He moved to the door with a heavy step. "Happy Thanksgiving, Mom. Enjoy your dinner. I'll be spending the day in the woods." He swung the door open, letting it bang shut behind him, punctuating his departure like an angry adolescent.

She let him go.

Thursday morning Annie snuggled Kyle as they watched the Macy's parade. Then they tackled preparations for a feast. Kyle sprinkled salt and pepper on the upright turkey breast, then watched, round-eyed, as Anne slid the meat into the oven. He mashed squash, then added butter and brown sugar until the color looked right.

"Cinnamon, too," Annie coached, smiling.

She peeled potatoes while he mixed Jell-O, stirring to dissolve the flavored sugar.

"I love red Jell-O best," he exclaimed. They ladled the Jell-O into fancy glasses before chilling it.

Stuffing from a box. With just the two of them, she'd never learned how to make good stuffing. There hadn't been much need. Still it seemed funny to use a box on Thanksgiving.

She set the gravy packet aside until the meat was done, and told Kyle the story of the first Thanksgiving like she did every year. Now Kyle was old enough to take pleasure in the tale. Understand the people.

They took a walk while the meat cooked, sporting bright orange vests to ensure visibility. Thanksgiving fell in the middle of deer season. Anne had no desire to court trouble; she simply wanted to hit the nature trails with Kyle. Gathering acorns and leaves, Kyle noticed the prevailing silence.

"In the spring," Anne assured him, "the woods come alive. Birds everywhere, singing. You can't sleep in the morning because the birds are so noisy. Building nests, getting ready for their babies. Rabbits. Deer. Possum, raccoons. Skunks. Mice and moles that scuttle everywhere. It's amazing, Kyle."

"Will we still be here in the spring?"

She nodded, refusing to think of reasons to flee. Somehow she'd get the courage to confront her past. But, how? When?

"Yes." She gripped Kyle's hand tighter. "I'm contracted for the year. I won't be done until the end of June. We'll make our plans then."

"Like the birds," Kyle asserted.

"Like the birds," she echoed.

They walked quietly, then Anne angled them home, into the wind, the trip back more of a struggle. Kyle squeezed her hand. "Do you miss Grandma?"

Quick tears filled her eyes. She hadn't been able to glance at her mother's room all day, knowing how she'd react if she let herself ponder the holidays missed, the time lost because she'd run off. *God, why am I such a chicken? Why don't I have the courage to do what needs to be done? To face Tom Baldwin and report his actions. Am I that worried about my own image, my own part in this whole mess? Help me. Please.*

She nodded. “A lot.”

“I’m sorry, Mommy. I didn’t mean to make you cry.”

Anne stooped. “It’s okay to cry when you miss somebody.”

“And God knows we miss her.”

Anne smiled through her tears, his innocence endearing. “Yes.”

Kyle nodded firmly. “Miss Garlock said so. She told me God’s taking good care of Grandma in heaven, that he wants us to be happy, but he knows we get sad when people leave and that it’s okay to cry.”

“Miss Garlock is very smart.” Anne made a note to thank the Sunday school teacher. Her simple explanation made sense to Kyle. Shoot, it made sense to Anne in a time where not too much had made sense lately.

Kyle clutched Anne’s hand tighter. “Will you go to heaven soon?”

Anne looked straight into his eyes. “God calls us when he’s ready, kiddo. But usually it’s when we’re old and tired.”

“Grandma was tired.” Kyle’s voice said that made sense.

“Yes, she was.”

“I miss Joe.”

Anne’s heart jammed. “What brought that up?”

“He used to talk to me about stuff.” Looking down, Kyle scrubbed a toe in the leaf clutter. “I just miss him.”

“We’ll see him around,” said Anne, her voice matter-of-fact while her heart clenched. She palmed Kyle’s head, meeting his gaze. “In the meantime, you’re stuck with me. Make the best of it, kid.”

Kyle grinned. “Race you to the mailbox?”

“You’re on.”

He won by an easy margin, then laughed at her antics as she puffed for breath. Slipping off their shoes, he noted, "Someday you won't have to let me win. I'll just do it."

Anne ruffled his hair. "I don't doubt it for a minute. Let's get cleaned up and finish dinner."

Once she'd tucked Kyle into bed, Anne curled into her mother's favorite chair and cried the tears she'd held back.

She cried for Kyle. For the grandfather he never knew, and for the father that chose to ignore his own child. For her mother, the time lost and the memories she cherished.

For Joe, a man whose impenetrable armor was pierced by her sinfulness and fear, her lack of courage.

Reach out.

Anne laid her head against the wing-backed chair, a fistful of tissues pressed to her face. Her heart thumped, haphazard.

Remember the woman who touched the hem of my garment? She found what she needed. Her faith healed.

I am with you, always. I won't let you fall. Reach out, Anne. Trust in me with your whole heart, your whole soul. I am the Alpha and the Omega. The beginning and the end.

Reach out.

The hem of His garment. The words echoed in Anne's brain. *I am with you always, the Alpha and the Omega.*

The hem of His garment.

Tentative, Anne reached forward, imagining that poor woman, a woman who'd bled for years, always tired, always worn, reaching out for love. For healing. Her trust pushed her through the throng where her faith saved her.

A gentle peace coursed through Anne, blanketing her. Her fingers moved. She imagined the courage of that woman, working her way through the crowd, ignoring laws that restricted her contact with Jesus, her belief urging her forward.

From faith comes courage. Anne reached for her mother's Bible, its worn cover dulled with dust. She grimaced at the simplicity she'd missed all this time.

Your word, O Lord, imprinted on my soul. Together, we can face anything.

Why hadn't she seen that before? She'd run, she'd hidden, she'd cowered in shame when all the while God reached for her, forgiving her. Loving her.

Her mother's words rang true. God had issued forgiveness long before Anne was ready to forgive herself.

It was time. Swiping her eyes, Anne made a decision. There would be no more running, no turning back. She would do what had to be done, no matter what.

Tom Baldwin was evil. She'd faced that evil as a child, her youthful emotions preyed upon to satisfy his lust. It was time others recognized the danger. Guarded against it. She'd meet with the sheriff once Kyle was in school. Spill it all, then deal with the aftermath.

Going public would be brutal. People who merely disliked her now would hate her for bringing Tom down. With so much time passed, there might be little to be done. But at least the information would undergo public scrutiny, Tom's evil revealed. Parents would be more watchful. With heightened awareness, Tom should find it impossible to take advantage of another young runner.

Maura's words resounded in Anne's ears. "Right is right." Regardless of outcome, Tom Baldwin would find a different adversary in a court of law than he had in that sun-dappled autumn wood.

And about time, too.

CHAPTER 16

Joe opened the office on Friday morning in no mood for nonsense.

He'd spent the holiday hunting, refusing to think about turkey, stuffing, gravy or Annie, none of them worth the bother.

A basket of food waited upon his return. The note taped to the handle read, "Hope the hunting helped. Walking is good therapy. So is prayer. Love you, Mom."

He reheated things, refusing to lament his choices, then smiled when he found pecan pie tucked in the corner. She must have made it after he'd stormed out.

Mothers. They smack you upside the head one minute, appease you with pie the next.

Her pie was almost as good as Anne's. He ate some while warming things, then realized he'd eaten a third of the dessert. Wrapping it, he'd tucked the pie away for the weekend before starting on his warmed-up dinner.

No doubt he'd given his mother's family something to talk about with his absence. He shrugged and moved to his desk, preparing to start a new day. Shifting things, he greeted Kim when she barreled in, sputtering how holidays were the least restful things known to man.

Mike stopped by, Etta Frank registered a complaint about her neighbor's dog, the local florist lodged one against a woman with two bad checks, and at one-seventeen, Jackie Ellers, former running star of Forest Hills Central High, walked in, flanked by her parents.

Joe rose, extending his hand. "Ava. John. Good afternoon. Jackie." He shook their hands, then shifted his look to John. "What can I do for you?"

John's dark face contorted in anger. Hands fisted, he met Joe's eye, his jaw tight. Motioning them to sit, Joe drew up a third chair for Jackie, then brought his from behind the desk. Settling into the seat, he offered them a look of concern. "What's going on?"

John leaned forward, clenching his hands. "We're here to swear out a complaint against Tom Baldwin."

Lawmen never showed surprise, except for their own gain. Joe regarded John, his emotions concealed. "For?"

John's look went to Jackie, her face pinched. "Rape."

The one word response hiked the stakes. Joe kept his look even with effort. "This is a serious matter." He eyed the family. "Shall we begin at the beginning?"

"That would be when I was in eighth grade," offered Jackie softly.

Joe's stomach seized. His jaw locked. The whole concealing emotion thing? Didn't work for about thirty seconds while Joe struggled to regain his bearings. "I'm sorry, Jackie. What did you say?"

"You heard her right," sputtered John. "Eighth grade and the pig took advantage of her."

Professional reason kicked in. Joe turned to the girl. "Let's take this to the back office. It's nothing we should talk of where people might come in. All right with everyone?" He stood.

"That would be fine, Joe." Ava stood first, her hand on Jackie's shoulder. "Let's go."

Walking back, Joe's mind raced, but the look he gave them in the private back room stayed calm with effort. He pressed a button. "Kim?"

"Yes, Chief?"

"Back office, please."

She arrived within seconds, nodding politely to the older Ellers. She gave Jackie a friendly smile. "Saw your fall stats. You're doing us proud."

The faint smile Jackie offered in return was a faded replica of the ones Joe knew as she grew up. Bright and energetic, with the legs of a gazelle, she'd been dubbed "the next Anne Kellwyn" by the locals. Her hard work earned her a full ride to Vanderbilt. She was about to complete her third semester.

"Jackie, I want Kim here so you'll feel at ease," Joe explained. "Talking about sexual things can be embarrassing. If you need to talk to a woman initially, Kim will be glad to take your statement. I can withdraw. Your parents are welcome to stay or step out as well."

"We're staying," declared John.

Ava laid a pale hand against the dark serge of her husband's Carhartt. "If Jackie needs time with Kim alone, we will, of course, accommodate her." Her eyes were soft upon her daughter, then hardened as she turned to Joe. "Whatever it takes, Joe."

He nodded. "Are you okay with me here, Jackie?"

She took a breath and clasped her mother's hand. "Yes."

"You said this started in eighth grade?"

Kim straightened. She was taking notes, as was he. They'd compare them later.

Jackie nodded again. "I stepped up to varsity in eighth grade. Coach made me feel really good. He kept talking me up, telling everyone how good I was. That I was one of a kind. Special." Her eyelids fluttered, blinking back tears.

Joe's hand stilled. Tom said the same thing about Anne.

Clicking back into the present, he nodded. Jackie drew a deep breath. Her lower lip quivered. He saw her physically shut the reaction down. Compress it, contain it. Again he was reminded of similarities to his ex-wife.

"He flirted with me, but I didn't mind. He flirted with everyone, teasing them. All the girls."

Joe knew the truth in that. Tom needed constant affirmation of his appeal.

"When I won the spring sectional title in the two-mile, Coach told me he wanted to celebrate. We went on a run together, up Adler's Hill, to where his family had a cabin above the creek."

Joe pictured the setting in his mind.

"Coach said he wanted pictures. Said he was a photo buff and these could be used on the cover of a national magazine. 'Jackie Ellers goes Division One' or 'Ellers signs with Michigan'. Things like that." Tears wet her eyes, but didn't spill over. She'd obviously had practice holding them in. "He had me do all kinds of poses, wearing my warm-ups. Then he wanted shots without them."

She went silent a long moment. Joe leaned forward. "And?"

Her hand twisted in her mother's. Her look swept down, then up. "I took them off."

Ava drew a breath. Her hand squeezed Jackie's in silent support.

"I was thirteen," Jackie offered in explanation. "Tom was the coach everyone dreamed of, that they longed to work for, and he went above and beyond with me. He was always encouraging, patting me. Touching me. Hugging me. I thought..." She paused, uncomfortable, shifting her gaze. "He made me feel cared for. Special. To have Coach Baldwin notice you meant you were something. And I *wanted* to be something." Her voice broke on the last word.

Joe leaned forward. "Honey, in eighth grade we all want to be something. That's natural. What happened after you took your warm-ups off?"

"He took shots from every angle, telling me how great I looked, how marvelous I would be, what terrific form I had. He'd be talking, then ask me to drop my shoulder, cock my head, give him a 'come get me' look." Jackie shook her head. This time a tear trickled down the smooth, beige skin of her cheek. "I didn't even know what a 'come get me' look was."

"I should hope not," sputtered Kim.

"He took pictures..." Joe led Jackie back gently. "Then what?"

Jackie kept her eyes downcast. Ava laid her cheek against Jackie's hair. The girl brought bright brown eyes back to Joe's. "He kissed me." She drew a breath and sat more upright. "He told me he loved me. Needed me. That he wanted me to take her place."

Joe frowned. "Her place?" He exchanged a glance with Kim. She shrugged. "Whose place, Jackie?"

"His wife's?" She shrugged. "I don't know. He kept muttering things while he held me, whispering things. And touching me."

"How did you handle that?"

She half-snorted, half-sighed. "I don't know how to explain it. There was a part of me that was almost honored by his love, as weird as that sounds." She darted a quick look to her father who nodded, his mouth set in a grim line. "Of all the people in the world, even his wife, Coach Baldwin loved me. Wanted to kiss me." Jackie shook her head at the childlike rationalization. "Then, when I realized what he intended, I got scared. I'd never thought of *that*," Jackie protested, hands twining, her forehead knit.

"That?" Joe prompted gently.

Jackie sighed. "Sex. The thought of making love with him never occurred to me, even when he was kissing me, but then he started touching me, and I..."

Her chin dropped. A tear fell dark against pale blue jeans.

Joe understood. “Sex is tempting because it’s pleasurable, Jackie. Those are normal feelings. Even at thirteen. What isn’t normal is for a man to covet a girl. It’s still considered rape because of your age, no matter how Tom made you feel.”

“But I should have known,” she insisted. “He took me to a deserted area, got me to shed my warm-ups, snapping pictures... I wasn’t dumb, Joe. And by the time I left there, I wasn’t innocent, either.”

Kim leaned forward. “A lot of kids confuse those feelings, Jackie. That’s why laws prohibit adults from preying on minors. They’re too young to weigh the consequences.”

Joe envisioned the area Jackie described. It was out of the mainstream, inaccessible without concerted effort. A great place to commit a heinous act.

Joe fought the sick feeling in his stomach. “What happened then, Jackie?”

She drew a deep breath. “He was real nice to me. He held me. Said I made him feel special. Then he told me there was nothing to cry about, because love was a beautiful thing, and that we should celebrate our feelings often.”

Tom Baldwin was lucky to be miles away right now. “What did you do then?”

“I went home. Took a shower. Hid in my room. I told my mom I was sick because I’d run too much in the sun. She believed me.”

“I had no idea,” Ava offered, her eyes filling. “I had no reason to doubt Coach Baldwin’s intentions. Anyone could see she was amazing. I thought it showed good sense that he saw it, too.”

Joe nodded. “How often did this happen, Jackie?

She hesitated, then hauled a deep breath. “Three more times over the next few weeks.”

“You never told anyone?”

"No. How could I? I knew what we were doing was wrong, but it felt..." She shook her head, her self-loathing obvious.

Joe nodded. "I understand. You never mentioned it to anyone, a friend, a boyfriend?"

Jackie shook her head. "No. I just tried to forget it happened."

"How did it end?"

She grimaced. Her hands twined once more. "I saw his wife one day, at the supermarket."

Joe nodded, picturing Jeannine Baldwin. Nice woman. Kind. Caring.

"She was pregnant. Very pregnant, and it hit me, what I was doing. After that, I wouldn't go anywhere with him. I avoided him. When he tried to talk to me, I clammed up. Then he just stopped."

"Really?" Joe sat back. The picture Jackie painted posed unusual behavior for a pedophile. Once they had you cornered, they used that leverage to use a victim frequently. Or kill them. If this allegation was true, Tom Baldwin followed a different profile. "You kept running for him," Joe mused out loud. "Why?"

Jackie's look flickered to her mother, then her father. Both looked guilt-stricken. The girl's chin quivered before she drew a deep breath. She studied her hands. "My mom was a runner. Before Title Nine."

Joe nodded. Anyone with sports knowledge understood how the landmark decision changed the image of high school and college athletics. The updated law opened a new realm for women, a dominion that didn't exist in Ava's day.

Jackie lifted her shoulders. "She never had the opportunity to be great. I did. I knew I could go places with my running. Even in eighth grade, I saw that. And Coach never touched me again. He treated me well after a bit. Went out of his way to be nice to me." Her face twisted, confused. Once again Ava's hand clutched her daughter's. John Ellers sat stiff, unmoving, his anger barely restrained. Jackie shook her head. “My dad was in China on business and my mom was busy with Maggie.”

Joe glanced at Ava. The look of remorse on her face spoke volumes. Maggie Ellers had suffered from leukemia during Jackie’s adolescence. Long since in remission, the girl’s life-threatening illness had strained the family fabric. Joe bit back a sigh of chagrin. If what Jackie said was true, Tom’s timing was perfect. But then, Tom Baldwin was a smart man.

“I didn’t know what to do,” Jackie went on. “I was scholarship material. I knew it. My parents knew it. Coach said I could have it all. Then, after what happened...” Her voice trailed, her face pinched. She blinked. Sighed. “I felt responsible. And guilty. Because I was,” she finished.

“You were a kid, Jackie.”

“But I wasn’t stupid,” Jackie insisted, as if eager to share the blame. “I thought I loved him,” she explained. “He made me feel good about myself at a time when I felt like I was disappearing into the woodwork. After a race he’d grab my shoulders, give me a hug, kiss my forehead, tell me how wonderful I was. How special. He treated me like I was the only girl in the room. I just never expected it to go that far, and when it did I didn’t know how to stop it.” She shrugged.

Joe didn’t doubt Jackie’s description. Tom’s eye for the opposite sex was well renowned, but this? Jackie Ellers was the reason laws against such things existed. Adolescent emotions could be preyed upon with little effort.

“I went with him willingly,” Jackie acknowledged. “I should have known better. Understood what he wanted. But I didn’t,” she insisted, her voice small, her expression tight. “Until it was too late.”

A hollow silence followed. Joe broke it, leaning forward. "Did he ever do anything else to you, Jackie? After that season?"

"No. He treated me normal, mostly. But every now and then he let me know he was glad to be my first."

Kim's fingers clenched. Joe put a cautioning hand against her forearm.

"How did he do that?" Kim asked.

Jackie's eyes flitted to John. He nodded, his gaze locked on the wall behind Joe.

"He would tell me I was exceptional, and that I made him feel the same way. That he never watched me run without remembering our special time."

Her words fueled the growing flick of anger in Joe's gut, but he constrained the emotion and nodded, face flat. "Yes?"

"Once he did it at an awards banquet."

"How, Jackie?" Kim leaned forward.

Jackie contemplated her fingers. "He called my name to present me with the award for female athlete of the year."

Joe nodded. It was big news to garner that award. Jackie received it three years running.

"He told everyone he was my *first* coach, and how proud that made him. That it was an extraordinary experience to help me develop. He told the whole room that he loved to look back at my earliest pictures, and see how much I'd grown up."

Kim snorted. Joe put up a cautioning hand and asked, "What did you do?"

"I cried. Everyone thought they were tears of joy, but coach knew better. He looked me straight in the eye when he said it, and all I could think of was what we'd done. His wife was right there at the front table, smiling up at me, and all the while..."

Mind control. Joe bit back what he wanted to say. Predators who were driven more by power than lust were the hardest to catch. They were unlikely to follow a precise pattern and smart enough to limit mistakes.

But this. This would divide the North Country into armed camps. Those that stood with their much-beloved running coach and those that would side with a young African-American, a girl whose beauty was as noticeable as her talent and brains.

A kid who'd had it all until Tom Baldwin abused her, six years before.

"You kept this to yourself a long time," Joe reasoned. "What brought you forward now? What's happened?"

She stared at him. "I can't sleep. I can't eat. I can't run. It's taken over my life." She raised her shoulders in silent surrender. "I tried to put it behind me. Deal with it. I never told my parents, my sister, no one. I figured as long as nothing happened again, I'd be fine. I wasn't pregnant, I had my whole life ahead of me. And Coach Baldwin was nice to me, like I was the sweetest thing on earth."

Of course he was, Joe thought in disgust. Using the child's feelings to keep her in place, feed the flames.

Tears slipped down her cheeks. "I thought if I could run fast enough to get a scholarship, I'd be at peace. All I wanted to do was get away from Forest Hills." She pressed her lips together, then shrugged. "Running was the best way to do that."

Kim handed her tissues. "It's affecting your life now?"

Jackie firmed her chin and faced Kim. "I have no life. I don't date, I don't talk, I barely function. I'm so angry that I just want to scream."

"When we found this out last night, we decided we'd get our girl to a therapist," offered John, his voice tight. "But we want justice done, Joe. Tom Baldwin has been lauded. People see him as a hero. Well, he's not. He's an abuser, and he will pay for what he did to my daughter."

Joe nodded. "I understand your feelings."

"You don't. You couldn't possibly," returned John. "The idea that someone we trusted could ruin Jackie's life makes me feel like a lousy father. My little girl ran for him, jumped through hoops for him, and lost her virginity to him, a man she should have been able to trust." He thumped a fist to the chair. "There's no way you could know how I feel, to know I let that go on without protecting her. Without making her realize her Daddy would do whatever it took to make things right."

Tears glistened in John's eyes. Joe's throat thickened in return. To see a big man like John Ellers brought to his knees because he couldn't protect his child... A humbling experience.

And horrifying in its implications.

Jackie's report was chilling in its audacity, its power-lust. Nodding, Joe got down to the brass tacks. "Jackie, I'm going to need some specifics. As best you remember them."

Jackie returned his look with one of abiding sorrow. "There's not a thing I've forgotten, Chief. Not that I haven't tried."

An hour later he bid the Ellers goodbye and rubbed a hand across the ache in his head. Kim poured him coffee from a fresh pot. "We'll be needing this."

"You can say that again."

A trip to the site revealed what he remembered. The seldom-used cabin had burned a few years before. Other than the old stone fireplace and remnants of the burned-out shell, the building had sustained a total loss. Set high on a knoll above the creek, the place had been nothing more than a rough-sawn, two room shack that acted as cover for cooking and sleeping. Not exactly a suburban getaway.

The fence Jackie described ran along the bank. Split rail, poor condition, but there.

The sights and sounds she remembered, the smell of old rubber?

Gone.

Joe scratched his head. This would be tough. Getting back to the office, he met Kim's eye. "Nothing. Building's gone, leveled except for the fireplace. Fence is there, but broken. Nothing else remaining."

"But others can corroborate based on their recollections," Kim answered. For a short time this morning she'd been pure woman. Not good. In America, people were considered innocent until proven guilty, and Kim had embraced the 'hang him now' mentality for long minutes after the Ellers left.

"We need evidence, Kim." Joe frowned, thinking. "The obvious thing would be to see if this was an isolated incident. If Jackie's story is true—"

"And I'd bet dollars to donuts it is," interjected Kim.

"Then there should be other victims. Tom doesn't fit the average profile, but—"

"Tom likes to be the best," noted Kim.

Joe agreed. "That's a big factor. We need to call in the big guys."

Kim scowled before she nodded acceptance. "You're right. It's not a competition and we don't have the manpower or the expertise to examine this properly."

"And the sheriff's department does," Joe agreed. "I'll call the detectives. You call the other guys and have them meet here. We've got to roll on this."

"I know." She clutched her mug, resigned. "Mike will hate working with them."

"Mike needs to be less territorial," Joe asserted. "Have them here by three-thirty. Might as well fill everyone in at once."

Sunday morning's edition of the North Country Herald carried the allegation. As Joe scanned the article, he set the paper back. "I would have liked a little more time with Baldwin unaware."

Detective Bill Masterson of the county sheriff's department shrugged. "Might be to our advantage. A case this cold, the news might shock Baldwin out of his complacence. Push him to make a mistake. Bring other victims forward."

Joe eyed him. "You leaked the story?"

Masterson nodded. "Yes. We'll work this from every angle to see justice done."

"And if he's innocent?" Joe raised a brow to the pair of detectives sitting in his office.

"Then a note of apology would be in order," answered Gina Rooks, Masterson's partner. "But it won't be necessary. Jackie Ellers is telling the truth."

"Woman's intuition?"

She shook her head. "Nope. Just seen it too many times before. She fits the profile of the abused kid too well. My money's on Jackie and her penchant to get on with her life. Put this in the past and forge ahead."

"Now what? Are you watching Tom, waiting for him to make a move?"

When neither answered, Joe sat forward. "You are?"

"Absolutely." Masterson tossed his foam cup away. "If he's got pictures, he might try to get to them. Destroy them."

"What if they're in his house?"

Gina shook her head. "Not likely. Wife, three kids? The chance of someone finding them makes that dangerous, and my bet is that Tom isn't after the danger aspect. He's totally in it for the ego. Someone to validate that he's still 'got it'."

Joe agreed. "You'll keep me posted?"

The detectives stood, shook his hand. "Yes. And we appreciate you calling us in before the waters got muddied."

"I hate passing things on," he admitted, letting his eyes meet theirs individually. "But more than that, I want this girl vindicated. I can live with the ego hit as long as you guys come through."

Rooks met Masterson's eye and nodded, extending her hand. "You can count on it, Chief."

Joe went to church in his uniform, knowing it would draw attention, knowing he had no choice because he was on duty. Eyes darted to him throughout the late November service.

The Ellers weren't there. They were seeing Jackie off on a plane out of Syracuse, sending her back to Vanderbilt for the four-week stint until Christmas.

That made them fair game, Joe surmised. He heard various comments after church, and knew few would have the guts to challenge him openly. Instead they'd align forces on one side or the other. At the moment, it was a run-away race, with Tom Baldwin firmly in the lead.

CHAPTER 17

"She led him on," declared one woman, her voice raised in indignation, her bulk preventing Anne's exit from Holy Trinity the Sunday following Thanksgiving.

"At thirteen?" The man alongside questioned the assertion. "She was a little girl."

"They mature faster than we do in *certain matters,"* replied the woman, her voice tart.

"Excuse us." Waiting for the group to shift, Anne nodded as she and Kyle eased by.

By the time she got Kyle to the door, she'd nudged her way through a lot of people. The pastor greeted her, his voice warm. "Anne, you're looking well. And this young man seems fine."

She nodded, an easy arm around Kyle's shoulders. "We're both well, Pastor."

"Thanksgiving went okay?" He clasped her hand. "Beth and I meant to stop, but Alva passed that morning and we spent a good share of the day with her family."

"We were fine, really," Anne insisted, tugging Kyle close as others approached. "But I thank you for the thought and prayers."

"You're welcome, child." His eyes dimmed as groups moved their way. "This is going to be ugly."

Anne frowned. "Because?"

He turned concerned eyes to her. "Your old coach has been accused of a heinous crime, Anne. The kind of thing that turns a town upon itself."

Anne reached a hand to the thick door, then worked to catch her breath. "Missy Volmer?"

The pastor's eyes sharpened. "Missy? No, no. You haven't read the paper."

Anne shook her head, relieved. If her

cowardice made her too late, she couldn't forgive herself. Not knowing she could have prevented it. "What has he been accused of?" she asked, the press of people edging her way.

The minister's eyes flicked to Kyle. "A crime against Jackie Ellers."

The sick feeling roared back with a vengeance.

Dear God, no. Not Jackie. Not Missy.

Not me.

The pastor turned to the gathering throng.

Anne stepped outside with Kyle. Fighting the wind, she steered him to the car, then drove to the nearest store.

The pastor was right. A bold-type banner declared a local running coach had been accused of crimes perpetuated on an adolescent girl six years back. It didn't take much to figure out the girl was Jackie Ellers.

Anne wanted to hit something. Break something. Take Tom Baldwin and—

Leaving Kyle at Sally's, Anne ran to vent her fury, hitting the trails with vicious intent, her chest braced against the north wind. The pressure felt good and terrible.

Why, God? Why did you let this happen? Is this my fault for not coming forward? Have there been others as well? Other young girls whose innocence was destroyed by Tom's lust?

Anger enveloped her. If she hadn't been afraid, Jackie might have been spared this whole experience. The violation, the degradation.

Why didn't I come forward? I could have prevented this. I kept quiet, trying to sweep things under the rug, and now he's ruined someone else's life. What's wrong with me? Why am I such a coward?

Loser, she taunted herself, pacing off the miles. *No matter how many times you cross that finish line in first place, you're a loser if you can't do the right thing.*

Finally spent, she headed for home and a hot shower. Once she was clean, she jumped in her car and drove to the Ellers.

John looked surprised to see her.

Not Ava. She took one look at the survivor standing before her and opened her arms. "Come here, baby."

Anne stepped into the embrace, feeling the older woman's hug as a gift from God. "I'm sorry," she blubbered, tears streaming, her body racked with sobs. "If I'd come forward, none of this would have happened."

"Hush, now." Ava's sweet voice floated over Anne, a quilt of comfort. "It's not your fault, child, any more than it was Jackie's. You saw evil and it scared you. Jackie, too. But everything's in the open now, and we will face this evil. Defeat it." Leaning back, she cradled Anne's face, her look full of sympathy, not recrimination. "We'll stand together, Anne. There's strength in numbers." At Anne's nod, Ava continued, "For surely, O Lord, you bless the righteous; you surround them with your favor as with a shield."

Wise words. Anne swallowed. "I'd like to call Jackie. Let her know."

John Ellers handed her his cell phone. "Here you go."

Jackie's phone rang three times before she picked up. "Hello?"

"Jackie?"

"Yes."

Anne inhaled. Ava clasped her hand, her touch reassuring. "This is Anne Kellwyn."

"Anne Kellwyn." Jackie's voice tightened. "I've always wanted to meet you. I chased your records a long time."

"And caught one of them," Anne acknowledged, the words catching. She breathed deep, trying to calm her racing heart. Once more, Ava squeezed her hand. "I'm calling about Tom Baldwin."

Jackie's voice softened. "Yes?"

Anne strengthened hers. "I'd like to help."

There was a pause before Jackie offered, "I don't understand."

Anne drew another breath. "Oh, honey, I think you do. I just wanted you to know you won't have to face this alone. I'll swear out my own complaint to bolster yours. We'll stand together."

"You mean...?"

"Yes."

Jackie started crying. "I'm sorry, Anne. So sorry."

Anne staunched her tears, wanting to be strong for Jackie. "I'm the one who's sorry. If I'd come forward, you wouldn't have been next in line. I was scared, Jackie. And embarrassed. My dad died and my mother was so sad, so torn up about that. I didn't want to make things worse for her. I just wanted to wake up and realize it was all a horrible dream and move on with my life."

"I know."

"This timing is so weird," noted Anne. "I'd just decided to come forward myself. I couldn't rest, couldn't find peace, then realized it was because I was living a lie. Until I cleansed myself, there would be no peace."

"That's it exactly," agreed the younger runner. She sniffed. "How did you get my number?"

"I'm at your house," confessed Anne, darting a watery smile to the Ellers. "Your parents were kind enough to hear my confession."

"This means a lot to me."

"Me, too."

"What now?"

"I'll see the sheriffs. Swear out a complaint. Go from there. He's going to have a tougher time fighting the charges of two."

"But it's so long ago," lamented Jackie. "There's so little proof. And a man like Tom Baldwin..."

"Needs to be punished," inserted Anne, calming. "We'll take it step by step. Okay?"

Jackie sounded relieved. "Okay."

Disconnecting, Anne turned to Ava. Her look of pride eased Anne's rise of guilt.

"You look done in," Ava noted. Glancing at John, she brought her eyes back to Anne's. "Why not stay with us tonight? It's not good to be alone when you're upset like this."

Anne gave her a hug of thanks. "As odd as this sounds, I actually feel better now that someone knows."

John stepped forward. "You never told anyone?"

"No."

"Not even Joe?"

Anne's heart fluttered at that thought. "No." She pondered the floor, then shrugged. "I think Joe would have a hard time understanding what kept me quiet. The mindset of a thirteen-year-old girl."

John worked his jaw. "I'm not sure you're right on that." As Anne reached for her coat, he reiterated Ava's offer. "You are most welcome to stay."

Anne gave them a tired smile. "Thanks, but I've got to get back. Kyle's at Sally Mort's and he's probably wondering where I've been." She hugged them both. "I'll call the sheriff's office first thing. Set things up."

"And I'll be right there with you," Ava promised.

"You don't have to—"

"Anne." Ava's voice broached no discussion. "Call me with the time, all right?"

Another weight slipped from Anne's shoulders at this bold show of support. Jackie's parents had every right to hate her, her silence allowing their daughter's abuse.

But they didn't. John gave her a bear hug. "We'll get him."

It was a guy-like phrase, but Anne appreciated the emotion. Their joint faith in her was humbling and exonerating. Anne nodded. "Yes, sir. We will."

CHAPTER 18

Joe maintained a presence on Sunday, knowing the curious and outraged would be out in force.

His instincts were spot on. No small number of people approached him, their voices soft in horror or raised in indignation.

The latter outweighed the former by a five-to-one margin. Jackie Ellers was in for a hard time.

By mid-afternoon, Joe needed a shot of normalcy. He headed to Boog's.

"You could probably use a good cup of coffee and someone who didn't want to yell at you about the travesty of a good man being brought down by a loose thirteen-year-old."

"I wouldn't refuse the coffee or the commiseration," Joe replied. He paced the store, eyeing this, touching that, then came to a stop in front of the oak rocker.

Finished. Polished. Completely beautiful. Boog had done a masterful job. The golden oak gleamed like candlelight, the soft luster of tung oil rich and full. The back grain ran free and wild, slipping to more demure striping on the wide, curving arms. The muted quilt invited repose. On impulse, Joe sat, testing the chair, his feet square against the braided rug.

"Comfortable?"

Joe shrugged. He wasn't sure if Boog meant the chair or him. "The chair is perfect. It fits. Some rockers don't curve enough to let you relax. This one is just right."

Boog nodded. "Good design. I've done others that weren't as user-friendly. This one works."

"I like the lighter stain on this one. A lot of my stuff is done in golden oak."

"Is it?" The nonchalant tone didn't fool Joe.

"Since you made my chairs, pretending ignorance won't work."

Boog sipped his coffee. "A lot of people like the lighter tones. Doesn't darken a room as much as deep-toned wood."

That was certainly true. When you lived where winter provided a steady presence, brightness mattered.

Joe rocked, the cadence of the chair relaxing him. After long minutes, he broke the silence. "This business will get ugly, Boog."

"Already was."

Joe acknowledged that. "How well do you know Baldwin?"

Boog shrugged. "He's been in the store a couple of times. Arrogant. Cocksure. Nice wife, though."

"Yeah."

"You gave it to the sheriffs?"

Joe nodded. "We don't have the proficiency to investigate things like this. They do. It made sense."

"But not easy."

Joe shrugged, staring into the flames. "Easy wasn't why I took the job. But who would have thought?" He didn't finish the sentence. Just sat, staring. Rocking.

Boog gave him a curious look. "Power-lust is a serious temptation, Chief. If these allegations bear out, there's likely to be more. I'm going to assume you've thought of that."

He meant Anne.

Joe stilled the rocker, his gaze trained on the fire. "Haven't thought of anything else. I sat listening to one young woman, hearing her pain, and all I could think of was how much she reminded me of Anne." He worked his jaw, his thumb rubbing the side of the mug. "Then I prayed the resemblance was because they were both gifted runners, not dual victims."

Boog stayed silent, then posed the question of the hour. "Would you have known, Chief? If Baldwin had...?" He arched a brow, his voice trailing.

The flames danced. Joe drew his brows together, thinking. Wondering.

Would he have known? Possibly not. For just a moment he cursed his innocence, the faith that kept him pure but inexperienced. He sucked a breath. "Not necessarily."

Boog read the look and gave a short nod. "You'll talk to her?"

"The detectives have a list of people to interview. Anne's name is on it." Joe's grip tightened at the thought.

"Her parents dead, no family to speak of." Boog's tone reflected his concern. "Not an easy thing to face alone."

"She won't be alone."

Boog nodded, his shoulders relaxing. "Glad to hear it. I always liked that girl."

"So did I."

Joe stopped by Anne's place later that day, using a cord of his seasoned firewood as an excuse.

No answer. He thought about leaving a note once the wood was stacked, but what could he possibly say on paper? "By the way, were you a victim?" No, he needed to see her in person. Talk with her. Watch her eyes, her body language, all the while praying what he feared couldn't be true, knowing it most likely was.

The thoughts that ran through Joe's mind put him in a precarious position. As a Christian he was taught to turn the other cheek. As a peace officer he lived under obligation to uphold the law, champion the rights of the innocent until proven guilty.

As a man he wanted to kill Tom Baldwin if what he suspected turned out to be fact.

Reconciling the three roles wasn't easy. The thought of Anne being molested made his blood boil. The realization that he'd been oblivious to it caused him shame.

He was a policeman, trained to spot victims. Identify them. Help them. Had he missed the signs in his own wife?

Sitting in the living room of the A-frame that night, he put his head in his hands, thinking.

Probably so. Anne had demonstrated the signs of post-traumatic stress. Worry and depression. Tears. Haunting dreams that wouldn't let her get a night's rest.

He knew he hadn't hurt her. Would never hurt her. But his pride had been so dented by her flight that he hadn't followed through the way he should have. He'd let her go, just like his mother professed, without going after her, searching for the truth.

Why? Why hadn't he swallowed his pride and followed his wife? His action then might have saved them years of tortured silence.

Maura's initial reaction confused him. She'd obviously thought him the guilty one, as in the dark as he'd been. Now her deathbed confession made perfect sense. For eight years she had protected her daughter from the wrong man.

You there, God? Pacing, Joe stepped onto the deck. *I know you don't hear from me as much as you should, but you know me, Lord. From day one, you've known me, even if I don't lay my problems at your door as often as I might.*

I'm in the glass dimly. Can't see much that's clear. I don't like the reflection I see of myself, and I have an urge to lay hands on another man. A very strong urge. I want to watch him suffer under the blows of my fists. To hurt him like he's hurt others.

What do I say to Anne, if what I suspect is true? Do I apologize for being stupid beyond belief? Oblivious to the pain my wife suffered? Her mental agony? What's the matter with me, anyway? When did it become all about me?

Eight years ago, he realized grimly. When the town banded together to support him, he'd swallowed their pity like aspirin. Wallowing in his self-righteousness, he'd let the martyrdom go out of control.

Now he would pay for his stupidity. Hindsight provided clarity, but a man who truly loved a woman would have pulled out all the stops. Shelved his pride, and gone after her? Soothed her. Helped her.

He hated himself. Or at least the self he'd been back then. Examining his conscience, he wondered if time had matured him enough to be a better man now. The kind of man Annie Kellwyn deserved.

Probably not, but he could try. Dialing Boog's number, Joe woke him. "Boog?"

"Who is this?" The sleep-riddled voice didn't sound happy.

"Joe."

"Ah." There was a moment of silence. "What can I do for you, Chief?"

"I want the rocker. The oak one. And the quilt."

Boog's response sounded carefully controlled. "All right. That's it? That's why you called me at twelve-seventeen?"

Joe hadn't realized the hour. "Sorry, man."

Boog replied as though restraining a laugh. "It's all right. I'll get them ready tomorrow."

"Thanks, Boog."

Boog's voice held a note of triumph. "You're welcome, Chief."

At nine-ten the next morning, Joe took a call from Detective Rooks. "Anne Kellwyn just phoned. She asked for an appointment. Wants to meet as soon as possible."

His heart sank. "When is she coming in?"

"An hour."

"I'll be there."

He walked into the Canton investigative offices with a heavy heart. A lot came clear to him in the last forty-eight hours, but much remained obscure. A part of him wished he didn't have to hear Anne's testimony, but a bigger part insisted on his presence. He may have withdrawn that support eight years before, but he'd give it now. Atone in whatever way possible.

He saw Ava first. He wondered at that, then noted Anne's nut-brown hair tumbling over the back of her London Fog. She looked professional as she scanned postings on a bulletin board. For a moment he wondered if he was on the wrong track, then she turned. Saw him.

The look on her face, a mix of shame and remorse, cut deep. Taking advantage of the surprise, he moved across the room and grasped her arms. "I'm here." He nodded to Rooks and Masterson's office. "You won't go through this alone."

"How did you know?" She whispered as her eyes searched his, a stab of determination behind the fear.

He raised one hand to her cheek. "Because Jackie acted like you did eight years ago, and it broke my heart to see how stupid I was."

Gina Rooks stepped out. She nodded to Ava, looked at Joe, then dropped her gaze to Anne. "Is it all right if the chief stays, Ms. Kellwyn?"

Anne let her head rest against Joe's navy wool for just a moment. His heart edged wider at that hint of trust. He brought a hand of comfort to her shoulder.

She turned and nodded, then took a step forward. "It's fine."

Ava moved forward as well. "Shall I stay out here, baby?" Obviously she'd adopted Anne in the last forty-eight hours. Joe looked at her in appreciation.

Anne shook her head. "No. If you don't mind, I could use all the support I can get."

Joe squeezed her shoulder. "You've got it, Anne."

They made an odd five-some. Head down, he held Anne's hand loosely, listening to the preliminaries, registering the surety of her voice, the strength of her resolve.

When they got into the nuts and bolts, he had to work to stay in his chair. Keep himself calm. A sudden rush of empathy for John Ellers took hold. The older man was right. There was no way to understand the emasculation wrought by not protecting the ones you love until it happens to you.

Christian or not, Joe needed to kill him.

"Chief, you want a minute?" Gina's voice cut into his thoughts. Anne turned, her eyes red-rimmed but level. "Anne's been handling this a long while, Chief," the detective continued. "It's okay if you need a little time."

Joe surged to his feet. Stalking out the door, they heard his fist connect with a row of gray metal lockers as he moved down the hall. Then, again. Anne cringed and stood. Masterson shook his head. "Give him a few minutes, Anne. He needs a chance to come to terms with this. Deal with it on a man's level. He'll be back."

Gina brought bottles of water. Ava clasped Anne's hand. They sat, talking of nothing important, until Joe reappeared.

He appeared angry but controlled. He walked into the room, set gentle hands on Anne's shoulders and gave a squeeze as he nodded to Rooks and Masterson. "We can continue."

Anne felt the warmth of his presence behind her. A shield of strength. His hands braced her, their message a pledge.

She told her story in clear, concise terms, fact by fact, day by day. When she got beyond high school, Gina stopped her. “Anne, you had offers from all over, is that right?”

“Yes.”

“So why, in light of what happened, would you pick St. Lawrence University? Stay here?”

Anne’s answer was simple. “Joe was here. And my mother. No matter how evil Tom’s campaign was, it didn’t change my love for them.”

Joe wanted to cry. Almost did. He squeezed her shoulders and felt her head ease back against him.

“Joe had just graduated from the academy,” she continued. “He had just begun his career and I didn’t want to mess that up. Or leave my mother. I was all she had.”

“Joe could have been in police work anywhere,” noted Masterson, eyeing her.

“Not if you know Joe,” Anne replied, her voice soft. “He loves the North Country. His family’s here, his friends. All the best fishing and hunting spots. The North Country is his domain.” She paused, considering. “I kept thinking that if I could put it all behind me, I’d be fine. Everything would be all right. It was wishful thinking,” she admitted, facing the detectives, “But I didn’t know that then. And maybe I could have moved beyond, except for the pictures.”

“Pictures?”

Anne nodded. “The ones Tom sent.”

“He what?” Gina’s voice took an upward note. Her look sharpened.

“The ones he took the first day. They made it look like I invited his advances. When he sent the first one, I panicked. I couldn’t believe he still had them, that he’d use them for leverage. What was the point?” Anne made a face. "I hadn't told anyone. We'd both moved on. He'd gotten married and had a baby daughter. But he sent the snapshot with a letter that said he loved me. Wanted me. That he'd never gotten over me."

Joe squatted by her side. "You have the letter?"

She nodded. "Yes. And the other one."

Gina honed in. "He sent two different letters?"

"Yes. One during my junior year in college. The other was—" Anne's voice caught. Her lips shuddered. She dropped her chin.

Startled by her sudden loss of control, Joe cradled her jaw, tilting her chin. "When did he send the second letter, honey?"

The endearment brought tears, but he didn't care. The look on her face reflected the expressions he'd seen the last weeks of their marriage. "Tell me. Please."

"After our wedding." Head down, she brushed her cheeks with the backs of her hands in a movement both childlike and heartbreaking. "He wondered how you'd feel knowing you weren't the first. He talked about how I flirted with him. Came on to him. The picture he sent made it seem so real. There I was, stretching and posing, hamming it up." She drew a deep breath and wouldn't meet Joe's gaze. "It looked like I invited whatever came my way. And a part of me did, on a kid's level. Knowing that, recognizing my part," she raised her gaze to Joe's, her chin lax, her eyes sorrowed, "I hate myself."

Joe felt like he'd been hit between the eyes. Dear God, what she'd gone through. With Tom. With him.

How many times had he proclaimed his happiness that she'd been his first in everything that mattered, and how pleased he was that it went both ways. That she'd come to him pure, ready to share the communion of their bodies and souls.

How could he have been so blind? He'd pushed her over an edge he hadn't known existed.

Dropping his head to hers, he held her, letting her cry. With a grunt of composure, Masterson passed tissues. “Was that when you ran?”

She nodded. “Yes. I couldn’t handle anymore. He had the power to ruin the most important thing God gave me. My marriage. I couldn’t sleep, couldn’t eat. Joe and I wanted to have a family, but I couldn’t function. How on earth was I supposed to take care of a baby when I couldn’t move beyond the latest threat? All I saw was my guilt. I couldn’t live with that anymore. And I was so afraid of what Joe would think of me. How it would hurt him.”

“And that’s why you never told anyone?” Masterson delved, needing answers. “Your mother? No one?”

Anne contemplated that. “If things had been different, I would have told my mom. She was strong and I know she would have done everything she could to help me.”

Joe nodded. He’d had first-hand experience with Maura’s protective side.

“Why didn’t you tell her?” Gina studied Anne as she waited for an answer.

“When I got home that day there was a neighbor waiting for me. My father had collapsed. She drove me to the hospital, but it was too late. He’d died. He took his last breaths while I was having sex with Tom.”

Anger knifed Joe. Stronger. Harder. And he hadn’t thought that possible.

“I couldn’t grasp it. What I’d done while my father lay dying. And my mother’s grief, her sadness. How she faced his death alone because I was with Tom. Part of me hated Tom and part of me loved him. I didn’t know which part to trust. She asked him to be a pallbearer at Dad’s funeral. A trusted friend that was having sex with her eighth-grade daughter. I couldn’t dump that on her, not then. And later, once it stopped, it seemed like things might be all right.”

“Until he sent the letters.”

"Yes."

Help her, Lord. Joe breathed the prayer as he watched Anne's face. *Give her strength. Help me show her your compassion. Your mercy. The things I denied her as her husband.*

"By the time the second letter came, I couldn't live with myself, much less my husband." She kept her eyes on the detectives, not Joe. Her hands lay clenched, the fingers straining white. "Joe was so good. So solid. He always did the right thing." She paused, then dropped her gaze. "I couldn't bear to have him know how weak I was."

Joe covered her hands, willing her to look at him. She didn't.

"Do you still have the letters?"

"Yes." She raised her chin, determined. "They're in a safe deposit box in Watertown. I figured if I ever got enough courage to fight back, I'd need them."

The exchange of glances assured Joe justice would be done. Anne's corroborating testimony, her obvious state of mind, and the physical evidence of Tom's controlling, abusive nature would push any lawyer into a plea agreement.

Masterson recovered first. "Can we collect those today?"

"I'd be happy to be rid of them."

Ava hugged her. "You're a brave woman."

Gina's voice echoed it. "Amazing." She stood and eyed Joe. "Chief, can Anne ride with you? We'll follow."

Joe slipped an arm of support around Anne's shoulders. Like there was any way he'd let her out of his sight until Tom was behind bars. "Absolutely."

CHAPTER 19

Knuckles white, Joe clenched the wheel as they drove. He worried the inside of his cheek like he always did when upset.

But once parked, he came around the hood of the cruiser, opened her door, and took her hand.

Anne hesitated. Angling his chin, he contemplated her, then squeezed her fingers, reassuring. "Let's go." They walked into the bank side by side, not touching, but Anne felt his shielding presence watching over her. Guarding her. Maybe caring for her?

The bank officer escorted them to a small room. He disappeared, then returned with a metal box.

Anne's arm shook as she maneuvered the small key. Joe reached to help just as the key engaged. He stepped back, allowing the detectives access. Drawing Anne with him, he kept her close.

She tried not to think of how nice that was. How perfect it felt to be looked after by Joe McIntyre again. How easy it would be to lean into the broad chest she knew so well, letting him share her burdens.

But she'd given up that right, so she kept herself rigid, chin up. No use adding insult to injury by dreaming of something that couldn't be, wishing for something long since gone.

Gina Rooks eyed the zip-lock bag. She cocked a brow of appreciation.

Anne shrugged. “I like cop shows. They’re always bagging evidence. I figured I should do the same.”

Masterson looked at Joe. “That your influence, Chief?”

Anne saw Joe glimpse a photo. His jaw stiffened. “Annie’s got a mind of her own. A good one.” His tone tightened with repressed anger.

Gina slipped the bag into her case. “We’ll get these to the evidence lab. Enter them into the file.” She eyed Anne. “You did good.”

Anne’s early adrenalin rush faded to foreboding. The inquisition. Prying eyes, wagging tongues.

And how would her principal react? To have the students looking at Anne, wondering all kinds of things, asking questions?

Her confession would bring things to mind that children shouldn’t need to contemplate. Maybe more than Redmond Academy could tolerate.

Would they keep her on? Quietly let her go? Tuck her into a back office where contact with kids was limited as if what she’d experienced might be contagious?

Joe’s hand gripped hers. “When does Kyle get home?”

His question brought a reality check. “Three-forty.”

He led her up the stairs as he eyed his watch. “We’ve got time to talk then.”

“I’m not ready for an in-depth discussion on the whys and why-nots,” she balked.

“Wasn’t the topic of conversation I had in mind. We’ll save that one.” Joe’s voice stayed tight but level.

“Great.”

He stopped and turned. Looked down at her. His eyes, normally so vibrant and blue, shadowed dark with anger, his face set in rigid lines. He seemed impervious to the brisk, cold wind while Anne drew her coat closer. “Right now I’d appreciate simple cooperation, Anne Louise. We’ll have our heartfelt discussion at some point in time. At the moment, my objective is keeping you in one piece."

She stepped back. "I don't understand."

"There are people who might take exception to the idea of Tom Baldwin being targeted again."

"Especially by me."

Seeing her shiver, Joe drew her to the car. "We've got some wonderful people in this area, Anne. Foolish ones, too. A few I'd consider dangerous when provoked."

"Kindly tell me how I've provoked them," she sputtered as he swung open the door.

"Get in. You're cold."

He'd left the car running, as was the custom once winter hit. Joe's car was his office, and you didn't turn off the heat to your office. The warmth enveloped Anne, but couldn't quite touch the cold within.

"Am I in danger?" Anne demanded, facing him.

"You're a prime witness in a felony case against a pillar of the community. A churchgoer whose wife teaches scrapbooking lessons." Joe stared out the front window, then turned. "The fact that he's a pedophile won't negate that to some."

"Of all the stupid—"

Joe nodded, but put two fingers over her mouth for quiet. "Yes. But knowing it's there, knowing these charges are difficult but provable with your little cache of evidence, puts us in the driver's seat. My hope is that Tom takes a plea and we end it there."

Anne tried to ignore the feel of his fingers against her mouth. The combined scents of soap and coffee lingering on his skin. The memories his touch brought to mind. She shifted to provide a buffer. The sight of him, angry and earnest, made her heart hammer. Because of that, she kept her voice deliberately cool. "Tom Baldwin will never cop a plea. He loves a fight, and he'll enjoy knowing Jackie and I suffer."

Joe put the SUV in gear. "We need to talk this out. Let's get some coffee, examine our options."

"Our?"

"Absolutely. I'm a peace officer sworn to protect and defend. I obviously did a lousy job of it eight years ago. Let's see if we can improve my record."

"Joe." Anne sighed, exasperated. "You did nothing wrong. I just..." she chewed her lip, searching for words, "couldn't handle all that went on. It sat too long, fermenting. Then it blew, and you were in the line of fire. But none of that was your fault. It happened long before we fell in love."

"Anne, my wife showed classic symptoms of post-traumatic stress." His tone stayed firm and flat. Almost clinical. "I was your husband, a man trained in victim detection, and I didn't see it because I was too wrapped up in myself to put you first. Go after you. Since we agreed not to have this discussion now," his eyes pierced hers, intense, "I opt we change the subject to something of a more immediate nature. Keeping you and Kyle safe."

Her face drained. "What do you mean?"

He steered the car onto the highway. "People do dangerous things when threatened. We'll talk about it once we're home."

He radioed Kim that he'd be out of service. Long minutes later they pulled into a winding drive, heading up. As they rounded the last curve, Anne sighed. "You built it."

"Yes."

"It's amazing, Joe."

The expansive A-frame had been their dream, a house at home with nature. Stained cedar siding blended with the trees beyond. The panes of glass marking the front of the triangle shone in the winter's light. The wrap-around deck, overlooking both the river and the ascending hill, offered a panoramic view.

Puffs of smoke came from the chimney, lending an aura of home to the park-like setting.

"You like it?"

There was something indefinable in the question. She ran up the steps, her fingers light against the handrail. "It's the prettiest thing I've ever seen," she declared. Turning, she saw his Adam's apple bob. "You've done well."

He shrugged. "It's a place to hang my hat." He unlocked the side door and headed to the kitchen. Anne wandered the front, marveling, then followed him. "And we're here because?"

"I wanted to be able to talk privately."

That made perfect sense considering the nature of the conversation. "Can I have tea, instead?"

He frowned. "I don't have any."

"Oh."

He started hunting through cupboards, banging the doors shut behind him.

"Joe, it's all right. Coffee's fine. Tea's just... soothing." She shrugged. "Southern influence, I guess."

"I guess." He looked discontented.

A flurry of misgiving rose in Anne's chest. She hadn't meant to cause him more angst. She just wanted a cup of tea. Pressing her lips together, she watched as he withdrew milk and sugar.

Once the coffeemaker stopped, Joe raised the carafe and filled his mug. His hand paused over her cup. "You're sure this is okay?"

She nodded, displaying a calm she didn't feel. "It's fine."

Eyes narrow, he poured her coffee, leaving room for milk. She fixed her coffee, then followed him to the great room.

The rustic beauty of the natural wood walls said North Country. A blue-stoned stove pumped enough heat to warm the whole place. Split wood stood along the wall, stacked neatly, ready to burn. The mantel held pictures. Mounted buck antlers hung on either side, both ten-pointers. A twelve point buck's head adorned the far wall, the glass eyes proud. With work she brought her attention back to Joe. "It's beautiful."

He'd watched her survey the room from a wide recliner. Motioning her to sit, he leaned forward. "I'd like you to stay with my parents for a while."

Anne frowned. "Awkward, at best."

Joe shook his head. "My mother would be thrilled. Given a choice, she would have kept you and farmed me out for adoption eight years ago. She's always loved you."

Anne studied her cup. Joe's gaze was too intense. Looking at him made her nervous. "But your dad is protective, Joe. He'd be uncomfortable with me there, and they probably don't want a six-year-old running around. Can't I just stay home? Improve the locks?"

Joe shook his head. "Too isolated. The woods back right up to the house, and it's an easy access kind of place. Besides..." He worked his fingers, eyes downcast, concentrating. "I'd prefer you have a man close by."

"You really think I'm in danger?"

He didn't mess around. "Yes."

"Joe." She hesitated, alarmed. "This is why I never came forward. There are so many people who won't believe me. They'll hate me for bringing Tom down. Small matter that he robbed me of my innocence at thirteen." Agitated, she rose, pacing the room. "What have I gotten Kyle into? He's just a little boy."

"He'll be proud of his mother for doing the right thing," Joe asserted

"If we live long enough to have him appreciate it." Anne couldn't hide the worry in her voice. She'd considered the possibility of retribution, but it had been a long shot possibility in her estimation. Joe seemed to think it more likely.

He glanced around, then brought his look back to her. "You could stay here."

The offer startled and tempted. To be with Joe, live with Joe, play house with Joe?

Anne grabbed hold of her emotions. "No. That wouldn't do." The idea of being there, using Joe's things, rinsing his whiskers out of the sink because he never remembered to flush them away himself?

No way could she play house with Joe McIntyre. She had way too much residual feeling going on for her former husband and absolutely no desire to have her heart broken again.

Or break his.

But he made a good point. A woman with a child could be compromised easily. A mother would do anything to save her young, and Anne didn't want to be put to the test. She drew a breath and walked to the big window. *Show me what to do, God. Light up my path. I know Joe's right, that it's not sensible for me to be alone right now. It takes a while for people to simmer down when one of their own has been targeted.*

But the idea of living under his father's roof scares me. She stared at the river's curve, the flow steady and sure. She brought one hand to the clean, tempered glass, considering her options. *I saw the look in Mr. McIntyre's eye. Joe's mother would be fine, but his father? I don't know how to defuse that resentment, the anger I caused in a good man.*

But to live here, without benefit of marriage?

Turning, she eyed the rugged policeman that had been her husband and lover for too short a time. The urge to go to him was strong. There was no way she could resist that pull, living under the same roof. Being honest with herself, she knew she wouldn't want to resist it.

That left little choice, really. Unless...

"If you run, he wins."

Joe had read her thoughts. She puffed out a breath, then leaned against the glass. “I know. It’s just...” She pursed her lips and turned, arms out, her hands spread-fingered. “I’ve only just gotten control of my life. Now it’s being wrenched away and that frightens me. Makes me worry I could lose the ground I gained.”

“You’re stronger.” He didn’t move toward her, but his voice was a beacon.

She answered its call, moving in his direction. “I am.”

“You can handle this, Annie. You’ve had to be tough for a while. You’ll do okay.”

She pressed her lips, then nodded. “Yes, I will.” Making her choice, she acquiesced. “Will you call your parents?”

Joe looked instantly more relaxed. “Yes, but I’ll run by there with you. Explain in person. Can you refill my coffee?”

Anne took the hint. He wanted privacy to talk. Reaching for his cup, her hair brushed his face.

He breathed her in, then raised one hand to the thick mass. A finger grazed her cheek. Stepping back, she stared at him. Met his eyes.

Oh, yeah. She’d be staying at his parents’ lodge. Or her mother’s home. Or in the car.

Anywhere as long as it wasn’t in her dream home, with Joe McIntyre as a roommate, looking far too good in his navy wool.

She studied the layout of the kitchen, affording him time. When she could no longer hear his low tones, she brought the coffee out.

“Thanks.” Joe nodded, his chin set, his eyes subdued.

“You’re welcome.” She returned the pot before adding milk and sugar to his cup. He smiled.

“You remembered.”

“What? Oh.” Frowning, she stared at his cup and the milk in her hand, then shrugged. “Habit, I guess.”

"Must be." The smile disappeared as quickly as it came.

"So." She made a face. "What now?"

"They're more than happy to help," he assured her, his voice even. "Let's get your stuff."

"Now?"

He nodded. "Yes. The quicker I know you're safe, the sooner I can get back to work."

She stood, startled. "Oh. I'm sorry. I didn't mean to keep you from things."

"You're not," he explained. "You are my work today." The flat tone made it clear that's all she was. "I should have said get back to the station. I have paperwork to do after the holiday weekend."

"Of course." She fumbled with her coat, pulling it down from the hook alongside the door. "I didn't mean to keep you, Joe. I really am sorry."

Strong hands descended on her shoulders, turning her. Dark blue eyes searched hers. "Can we *not* spend the rest of our lives apologizing? I'm already tired of it."

She couldn't have shifted her gaze if she tried, and she didn't. Just stood there, staring at him, feeling the grip of his hands along her shoulders. The steadiness of him. Rock-solid. Wanting more than anything to step into those arms, she stepped back, creating a distance. "That's a good idea."

He nodded, then let go of her shoulders. Was that reluctance she saw in his eye? A disinclination to let her go?

But he did let her go. Grabbing his jacket and gloves, he strode to the door, opening it as he fastened the closures along his chest.

She used to tease him about being Dudley Do-Right in his uniform. The proximity to the Canadian border gave the joke more punch. Dudley was always running off to save Nell from the dastardly deeds of Snidely Whiplash.

But the cartoon had long since lost its audience and Anne was now faced with a real-life scenario. Joe, looking out for her, willing to sacrifice the peace of his family to keep her safe. Kyle safe.

For the moment, she'd take what she could get. His protection was nothing to scoff at. The man was a deadly shot with years of tracking experience, second only to his daddy. Having the McIntyre men cover her back wasn't a bad idea at all.

Just really awkward when one of them was the husband she'd sworn to love all her life.

And did.

CHAPTER 20

Suspended, with pay, pending an investigation. The words rang in Tom's ears as he strode out of the Forest Hills district offices. His fingers twitched, then clenched before he consciously relaxed them.

A bunch of suits. Wearing bad ties, besides.

Voting in emergency session, the Forest Hills School Board...

Which meant Joe McIntyre and company. What a sham. He could name three members of that board who'd never gone to college. Leave it to Forest Hills to elect the proletariat as their able representatives. A bunch of farmers and shopkeepers, who had no idea what it took to build winning squads, season after season.

What did they expect? For nearly twenty years, he established an unquestionable record. High passing rates on the Regents science exams. County running titles. Sectional championships. State medal winners in both cross-country and track. The trophy case in Forest Hills High offered silent testimony to *his* hard work, *his* endeavors. Was there another Class D coach in New York State who boasted such prowess?

No.

Did they think he'd let it slip away on the hysterical words of a nineteen-year-old? Not in this lifetime. He had plenty of evidence to show Jackie led him on.

What was a man to do? He was only human, after all. Not made of stone.

Jeannine. His wife's reaction had Tom raking a hand through his hair.

Megan. Brandon. Little Rory. His kids wouldn't understand what he'd done. How his choices affected them. Megan was willowy, like her mother. A born runner, like her father. Already he'd been grooming the eleven-year-old in the disciplines of distance running, and she was good. Very good.

Brandon.

Tom cringed, picturing his son. Brandon had a giving nature, like Jeannine's. His competitiveness was softened by an anxious-to-please personality. Another Jeannine trait. How would the nine-year-old handle this?

He'd hate him. His boy, his only son, would be ashamed of him, disgusted by his very own father. The thought of Brandon's eyes, wide with disappointment, haunted Tom.

He'd wanted to be a good father. Hadn't he worked hard, made a good living, taken them to church each and every Sunday? They had their own pew in Grace Chapel. No one sat in Tom Baldwin's pew, except the Baldwin's. No one.

Reaching his car, Tom pounded the steering wheel, frustrated.

Things should have been easy. Could have been, too, if Anne had followed the plan. But, no. She'd ruined everything by taking up with Joe McIntyre. Spurning Tom's advances. How patient had he been during her high school years, lingering on the edge? Anticipating the future?

A future Anne ruined with foolishness. He shook his head, distraught.

If she'd waited for him, none of this would have happened. There wouldn't be a marriage to Jeannine, or a liaison with Jackie. None of it would have been necessary if Anne played her part.

But she didn't, and now the Ellers girl was pointing fingers. She'd probably been with a dozen men over the years, but had the audacity to accuse him. Tom's breath grew ragged, remembering.

She hadn't even been a suitable replacement.

Slamming the door, he thrust the key into the ignition and made a swift turn, his heart pounding. *Great.* Just what he needed. Another heart attack. Willing himself to calm, he coasted to a stop at the juncture of Route 11, eyeing his choices. The lawyer's office in Potsdam, or Anne Kellwyn's bungalow on Old Orchard Road?

Old Orchard Road won.

As Anne gathered personal items, Joe lugged clothing and suitcases to the back of the SUV. Together they loaded Kyle's toy box, a corrugated cardboard discount-store type, laden with prehistoric creatures, cowboys, soldiers and spacemen.

"An eclectic kid," Joe noted, smiling.

"A boy." Anne rolled her eyes and grinned. "He's not above having the space guys ride herd on the dinos, either. I think I'm raising a science fiction writer."

"A good imagination's a kid's best playmate," Joe asserted. "Anything more you need right now?"

"I'm sure there is but it escapes me. When I'm at your parents and realize I forgot my pajamas—" She blushed and Joe was tempted to tease her. Flirt with her.

He shut the feeling down. Anne was in his protection, a protection he hadn't offered before. She'd be vulnerable now. He had no right to take advantage of that.

But later? When the ugliness of this business lay behind them? Just maybe—

His heart lurched. *Whoa, boy. One step at a time. Let's keep the lady out of harm's way, okay? First things, first.*

She'd looked so natural at his place. Making coffee, wandering the room. He understood instantly why it never seemed right to entertain women at his home. What had been missing all those years.

Anne. He'd built the house for her and it had waited, all this time. Just like him.

She'd been right to refuse his offer. In his heart she was still his. His wife, his woman. His lover.

But in reality she wasn't, and toying with that kind of temptation wouldn't be wise. Luckily she'd refused, probably amused he'd offered at all.

Unless she longed for him the same way. Two souls, destined from birth. Wasn't that how his mother saw them?

Joe bit back a sigh and climbed into the SUV. Fastening her belt, Anne glanced to her watch. "We need to pick Kyle up by three-twenty. That's when the buses pull out."

He nodded. "Have the school hold him, then I'll pick him up while you get settled, all right?"

She breathed easier. "That would be good. I don't want to mess his life up completely."

"Can't we just tell him you guys are taking a vacation at the lodge? That way he thinks it's an adventure."

"But shouldn't I warn him?" Anne scrunched her forehead, thinking out loud. "What if someone tries to hurt me through him? Shouldn't he be aware?"

"How about this," Joe proposed, shooting a glance to her. Even in profile she was pretty. An angular chin, straight nose, the sweep of her eyebrow arched. The girl had been lovely. The woman was stunning. "I can give the 'stranger danger' talk at school. I could schedule it for tomorrow, so Kyle won't know he's targeted. Jolie Evers usually does it with me. Jolie

Thompson, now," he explained. "Married, three kids. She's a school psychologist from Canton."

"I kind of remember her," admitted Anne. "Not too tall, dark curly hair, bright smile?"

"Yup."

"Your age, right?"

"Ouch."

Anne laughed. It was nice to hear. She hadn't done too much of that. He couldn't help but smile in return.

"I meant our paths wouldn't have crossed in school," she told him. "And you're not doing too badly, Joe." She appraised him, amused. "There's not a hint of gray and your face is unlined. Except for those cute laugh lines around your eyes."

"First I'm old, now I'm cute. Make up your mind, Anne."

"Luckily the two aren't mutually exclusive," she shot back. "And guys get to be both for much longer."

"Really?" They paused at a stoplight, and he sent her a look defying her comment. "If anything, you've only grown more beautiful, Annie."

Her mouth opened, surprised. He let his eyes linger there, then eased the cruiser forward.

"Joe, I..." Her hands fluttered, then twined.

"The proper thing to do when one receives a compliment is say 'thank you'."

She swallowed hard. "Thank you."

He nodded. "You're welcome. See? Wasn't so hard."

From the look on her face, a mix of pleasure and surprise, he saw it was, but that was all right. He hadn't become a trophy fisherman without learning the rules of gaming. Tease with the bait, jerk the line, then ease them in your direction. Make them think it's their choice.

Not that Anne was a fish, but the principle wasn't much different. If she decided to come back, he wanted her, heart and soul, but he wouldn't chase her. She'd run of her own accord and needed to return the same way. But he had no intention of making it any too difficult.

They picked up her car in Canton, then drove to the lodge. Once there, he toted things into the main building, sensing her awkwardness. His mother hurried across the living room, chatting brightly, grabbing items to lighten Anne's burden. "I've given you rooms on the south side, where it's brighter in December. Is that all right?"

Anne's expression showed her gratitude. "It's wonderful. I'm so grateful for this, Mrs. McIntyre. More than you know."

Deb shot her a sharp look. "Mom, to you. You haven't called me Mrs. McIntyre in a long time. I see no reason to go back now. Got it?"

Anne flushed, then nodded as they moved upstairs. "Got it. You sure you're ready to have a little guy running around?"

"More than ready," Deb retorted, bumping the door open with her hip. She sent a look of frustration Joe's way. "But this one's been moping around waiting for you, and Greg's just starting his practice, so I wait. Not very patiently."

"Mom." Joe gave her a look meant to quell. It didn't. She flashed a smile, then hustled back to the kitchen. He put a hand on Anne's arm. She looked up at him, an endearing smile tugging her mouth.

"I haven't been waiting," he grumbled, setting down an armload of hangers.

"Good."

"I just don't date a lot."

She turned more fully, her gaze locked on his. "Me, either."

"Well." Uncomfortable, he shoved his hands into his pockets. "You okay for a while? I want to get the rest and see Mom and Dad. Fill them in."

Anne glanced around. "I've got plenty to keep me busy. Do you need help?"

He shot her a look of bemusement. "Help. Right. I've been lugging things up these stairs for thirty years. I'm good."

She smiled again. "Thank you, Joe." In that smile was the image of the girl he'd married. The curve of the mouth, the sparkle in the eye. It was a sheen he noted when she looked at him. Deeper, brighter.

He straightened, then gave in. Reaching out, he pulled her into a hug and held tight, letting his strength, his warmth flow into her. One arm wrapped her waist, the other cradled her head. He felt the silk of her hair against the rough of his fingers. Breathed the scent of sweet almond on her skin. He couldn't find words to say what he felt. That he was sorry for her predicament, sorry for the past. Wasn't he the one who asked for no more apologies?

But he wanted her to feel safe. Comfortable. Holding her gave him the sense of both. He hoped it worked in return. Pushing back, she stepped away, chin down. "Don't be nice to me."

He sensed the tears before he saw them. Angling his head, he brushed them away with the pads of his thumbs. "I think I like being nice to you, Anne. Now." The emphasis on the last word was tinged with humor.

That made her smile through the tears. "Joe."

"Shh." He cradled her face, amazed at the flood of memories inspired by that simple touch. "I'm feeling altruistic, and there's no telling how long that will last. Let's just enjoy the feeling while it's there." Stepping back, he eyed her. "I'll be back."

She nodded, chewing her under lip in consternation.

He wanted to kiss her. Noting her uncertainty, the emotions roiling inside, he longed to kiss away the hurt. Shelter her.

With a grimace he came back to earth. Protecting her was the order of the day on a professional level. Right now, separating the professional from the personal was not working. Time for space. He backed up, then turned and strode out the door.

Finding his mother in the kitchen, he cocked a brow. “Where’s Dad?”

“Right behind you.”

Joe sent the older man an admiring look. His father’s knack for moving silently was at a level Joe had never achieved. He felt like an ox alongside the smaller man when they scouted a field.

His father lifted a brow. “What’s going on?”

“Let’s sit.” As he explained the circumstances surrounding both Anne’s disappearance and re-emergence, his father’s anger escalated. At one point he rose, strode to the counter and gripped the granite. Joe understood the emotion.

“Why didn’t she tell someone?” Turning, Jim’s gaze bore into Joe’s.

“Same reason as Jackie,” Joe replied. “They were kids; they thought they were in love with him, that they invited his attentions. He made them feel responsible while he fed their teenage crushes.”

“Were there others?”

Joe shook his head. “Don’t know, yet. We’re checking. Tom doesn’t fit the typical profile.”

His mother touched his arm. “What can we do since murder isn’t an option?”

Joe didn’t try to hide his agreement. “I need her safe,” he explained, nodding toward the stairs. “The boy, too. People won’t take kindly to Anne being involved. A lot of that is my fault for letting their anger with her get out of hand.”

Deb disagreed. “It’s not your fault any more than it’s Anne’s. People are people. Some good, some bad. They’ll come around. The folks up here are mostly the God-fearing, hard-working sort.”

“Who take their sports way too seriously,” Joe argued. “You know how people respect Tom. They kowtow to him, cut him deals no one else would get, give him free meals. All because he knows how to develop winning teams." Joe ran a frustrated hand across the buzzed hair at the nape of his neck. "The price that two young girls paid will seem like small change to some."

His father agreed. "You're right. There's already talk of Jackie leading him on, developing early, being a temptation." He shook his head. "As if a girl can help that her body changes at puberty. Right now I'd like to get my hands around Tom Baldwin's scrawny neck and give him reason to have another heart attack."

"Jim." Deb stood and went to him. "It's in the hands of the law. And God."

"I know that." Jim McIntyre's frustration mirrored Joe's. "But I also know how I feel. What kind of a man wouldn't feel that way?"

Joe agreed, rising. "I know. In my less lucid moments I've imagined ways to do him in. Make him pay the way Anne has for fifteen years. To hurt him and have him suffer like Jackie does now. Then I realize that no matter what happens, from this point on, Tom will be in pain. His family will endure a great deal for his sins. I hate that." Joe shook his head in dismay. "But it's not my fault. He bears responsibility for what he's done, and for what it will do to that nice wife of his. Those three kids. Tom will pay, Dad. We've got enough evidence to force his hand because he got power hungry with Anne." Thoughtful, he raised his eyes. "The less sensible part of me still wants to kill him. I just can't let that part loose."

Jim McIntyre strode across the room. He wasn't a hugger. Never had been. But this time he pulled his son into his arms, hugging him fiercely. "She'll be safe here."

Joe returned the embrace, then stepped back. "I appreciate it." He eyed his watch. "I've got to bring in the rest of her stuff and get to school for Kyle."

His father grabbed a woolen jacket and headed to the cruiser. "Let's go."

"Is Mommy there?"

Joe heard Kyle's note of indecision as he aimed the police cruiser toward his parents' lodge. "Yup. You guys are going to have a vacation at my mom and dad's place. My dad is a great hunter."

"Like the one who killed Bambi's mother?" The already timid voice went a distinct note smaller.

Joe grimaced. In the North Country, no one watched Bambi. The Disney classic bordered on profane in local circles. He weighed up his options, then offered, "Up here, people don't like to hunt for doe. Girl deer," he explained, glancing across the seat to catch Kyle's eye. "We hunt for males with a rack."

"What's a rack?"

"Antlers on the top of their heads."

"Like Rudolph?"

Joe couldn't win for losing. "Oh, we never hunt reindeer." He shook his head for emphasis. "They're special. They don't live around here, anyway. I'll show you what I mean once we get inside."

Anne stood waiting at the door. The boy was comforted to see her, but shrugged when she asked how his day went.

Deb laughed. "This is why God invented daughters."

Joe looked at her, affronted.

"So mothers will have someone to carry on a conversation with," Deb spouted. "Something unlittered with grunts and groans."

Anne commiserated. "That is so true."

Joe turned to depart. Anne paused, her hand in Kyle's. "You're leaving."

The hint of wistfulness in her voice had Joe gripping his hat tighter. "Paperwork that won't wait. Kim's been holding the fort all day."

Anne forced a smile. In return he made his look more assuring. "Are you settled in?"

Her smile said yes. Her eyes held a different message. "Just fine. Joe, I—" She stepped forward, her brow knit.

"It's okay." He backed toward the door. A long moment of silence followed.

"I've made venison stew and fresh bread," announced his mother, glancing from one to the other. "Are you coming back for supper?"

He didn't usually. Out of the nest meant out in his book, although he had no problem showing up for his mother's famous Sunday dinners. The woman could cook anything his father caught, netted or bagged. He almost shook his head, then caught the look in Anne's eye.

She seemed nervous. Oh, she'd do fine, sure. But, still... "I'll come back around six-thirty. That good for you, Mom?"

"Fine with me." Deb sent an innocent smile Anne's way. "How about you, dear?"

"It's fine with *me*," offered Kyle, oblivious to the silent interchange. "Can we play dinosaurs?"

"If you're good," Joe bribed. "And eat your dinner."

"Do I like it?"

Anne smiled. "Joe's mom is a real good cook, so I bet you do. We'll see, okay?"

"It smells good," Kyle offered, swinging his backpack. "Where are we sleeping?"

"Up here." Turning, she reclaimed his hand and led the way up the stairs. Joe watched until she disappeared.

"You were leaving?"

His mother's voice broke into his thoughts. He ignored the laughter in her eyes. "I'll be back in a couple of hours." He knew that meant long hours at home, catching up later, but he didn't want Anne uncomfortable. If it made her transition easier to have him around, he'd be around. After all, playing dinosaurs wasn't exactly a hardship. Or watching Anne grow sleepy by the fire. Imagine—

He stepped outside. The knife-iced air shortened his fantasies. Dreams that included a rocker and a quilt. Pecan pie. A wife to hold in the frigid nights of a North Country winter.

Dreams of a woman who would probably run from St. Lawrence County once she had the chance. Head south where the weather lay gentle and people accepted her.

St. Lawrence County didn't have much to offer Anne. Her mother gone, her father long since buried. No home to call her own. No friends to speak of. Most of Anne's crowd had left after college. That left nothing for her to cling to in Forest Hills, except Joe McIntyre.

But he could make it enough if she let him.

CHAPTER 21

Bill Masterson phoned Joe late that evening. "We've arrested Baldwin. The D.A.'s office is asking a stiff bail, citing him as a distinct threat."

"You're keeping him up there, right?" No way did Joe want Baldwin in one of his cells. He didn't trust himself around a man who sullied adolescent girls, one of whom was Annie.

"Yes. If he makes bail, which I'm sure he will, I'll let you know."

"Thanks."

"Joe?"

"Yeah?"

Masterson drew a deep breath. "They arrested him outside Anne's place."

The chill that swept Joe had nothing to do with the temperature. "He was there?" His brain spun the time frame. There was no way Tom could know of Anne's complaint. Her involvement had been kept quiet for that very reason. "Today?"

"He pulled off the road about a quarter-mile north of the house, late afternoon. The deputies waited until he breached the back door, just before dark. The door needs work."

Joe's hands itched for payback. "Don't let me near him."

"I hear you. When he makes bail, Chief—" The detective's voice held a note of warning. Obviously the other man understood Joe's feelings.

"Keep him in Potsdam."

The detective grunted. "I would if I could."

Arrested at Anne's. Joe balled his hands, imagining the possibilities. Anne, *his* Anne, alone with Kyle, would have been at Tom's mercy.

Why, God? What's going on here? Why does Baldwin target her? Hasn't she been through enough?

Is it convenience? She's here, and Jackie's in Tennessee? For a moment, Joe thought like the cop he was and not the husband he'd been. *What is it about Anne that makes her his objective? There's no way Tom could know of Anne's visit to the sheriff's office. Not in that time frame. Then, why?*

No answers came. He decided to keep the details of where Tom was arrested to himself, at least for the time being. Some things Anne didn't need to know. Not yet, anyway. She was safe at his parents' lodge, the flow of hunters providing good cover. Tom Baldwin might consider Anne fair game on her own, but no one in the North Country trivialized Jim McIntyre's prowess with a gun.

I wasn't going to hurt her.

Tom stared out the window of his attorney's car, sorting through details of the past forty-eight hours. The lawyer's voice droned, advising Tom's complete silence. "Pretend you're wearing blinders, Tom. You don't look left, you don't look right. Give me time to see what I can do. With the Kellwyn woman's evidence, things aren't looking good, but I'll do my job. See if I can discredit her."

Does he think I'm stupid?

Tom nodded, pretending agreement. He turned back, staring at nothing.

He loved Annie. Always had. Always would. It had nothing to do with sex, and everything to do with her. Couldn't they see that? When something was so perfect, so right, everything else paled in comparison.

And now she'd turned against him.

Hadn't he cared for her throughout high school? He'd never laid another hand on her, wanting their wedding to be a celebration of memories. He'd guided her, advised her, been the driving force behind her success, for what? So that she could get starry-eyed over some young cop? A kid who could never love and cherish her like Tom did?

Anger consumed him. A flash of his wife's face at the side window sliced his heart.

Jeannine. What could he say to her? *Sorry, honey, I never loved you? I married you because I wanted a wife. A showpiece. An attractive mother for my children?*

She'd fit the bill. Still did.

But she wasn't Annie.

The kids. Tom's heart skipped a beat, reality looming. He'd have to face them, see the revulsion in their eyes. The distrust. Not Rory, of course. She was too young. But Brandon and Megan? They'd hate him.

The lawyer parked the car. Tom didn't move. Staring at the house, he pictured the family inside, whose lives would never be the same after this day.

Funny. He'd always meant to make more time for them, but season by season, the years slipped by. Spring track, summer running camps, cross-country in the fall, and a winter track schedule that rivaled Division One colleges. On top of that, someone had to make a living. It certainly couldn't be left to Jeannine.

But it would be.

The reasoning made perfect sense. A man knew his limitations, and Tom Baldwin was no fool. State prison was not on his list of options.

With quiet decision, Tom stepped out of the car, squared his shoulders, and approached the steps, his attorney following.

Masterson called Joe. "Tom's out."

"Great." Joe wanted to kick something. Instead, he uttered a silent prayer for patience.

"You tell Anne yet?"

Joe exhaled slowly. "Tonight."

"How will she handle it?"

Joe had no idea. The thought of Tom lurking outside her door, waiting. Watching. If she was smart she'd run as far and fast as she could and never look back.

"We may have another one."

Joe tightened his grip. "Another victim?"

"Possibly. A girl named Adriana..." Joe heard the shuffle of papers before the detective continued, "Wellinger. She was a student between Anne and Jackie. Showed great promise, then left abruptly her eighth grade year."

"You're tracking her down?"

"Gina's on it."

"Good."

"You heading to see Anne now?" Masterson's voice was gruff but understanding.

"Yes."

The detective drew a long breath. "Good luck, man."

"Outside my house?" Blood drained from her face and pooled somewhere near her feet. "He found out I went to the sheriff's office that quickly?"

"No." Joe shook his head, studying her, concern shadowing his features. "He didn't know."

Anne found herself trapped in what-ifs, imagining what might have happened if she hadn't listened to Joe. Taken his advice.

But you did.

She grasped his hands. "Thank you."

"For?"

She swept the lodge a look. "Bringing me here. Keeping me safe. Watching out for us. Who knows what might have happened if we'd been there."

"But you weren't."

"Because of you."

"I need you safe, Anne."

She released his hands and took a step back. "For my testimony."

Joe stepped forward. "That's one reason."

She heard the words and the hint of teasing, but ignored them. Getting too friendly, too comfortable would be a mistake. A big mistake. And if Redmond let her go once they realized her involvement in this case, she'd be a free agent, ready to flee. She could always return for her testimony. She wasn't foolish. She knew how people would react to her added charges against Tom. No way would she subject Kyle to their heightened negativity. A boy deserved a chance to grow up unfettered by gossip and slander, right?

Joe laid gentle hands on her shoulders. "It will be all right. I promise."

Anne nodded half-heartedly. Joe was strong, but this was one promise he couldn't keep. No one person controlled the actions of a whole town. She knew that better than most.

Joe's phone rang at five-twenty the following morning. "Chief McIntyre."

Masterson's voice crackled. "Baldwin took his own life last night. His wife found him in a basement storeroom. According to the responding officers, it looks like he kicked the stool out just after she went to bed."

"Dear God." Joe could only imagine Jeannine Baldwin's horror at finding her husband, on top of discovering what he'd done. Who he really was. "How's she holding up?" His heart broke that such a nice woman would hold the bag for Tom's misdeeds. Three kids, no job other than helping nice folks chronicle scrapbook memories of their lives for their children. *Why, God? Why would he do this to her? To his kids?*

But then, why did Tom do anything? So used to winning, the idea of losing must have loomed intolerable. Of all the weak-spined...

Joe sighed. "Who's with her?"

"Tom's family."

Joe snorted. Peas in a pod, those Baldwins. All but Lara, Tom's youngest sister. An 'oops' baby old Tom called her, from his second marriage, but the girl was a peach. None of the Baldwin arrogance prevalent in her older half-brothers. He wasn't sure where she'd gone after college, but she had enough brains to stay there, minimizing the Baldwin effect.

"Jeannine's people will arrive later," Masterson reported. "They're from Albany, so it'll be a few hours."

"I'll make sure not to nab them if they hurry through town," noted Joe, one hand rubbing his chin. "This bites."

Silence descended as each man envisioned damage control. Tom's wife, kids, family. His teams of devoted young runners. Students, faculty. Once again Joe swiped a hand across his face when a thought struck hard.

Anne. And Jackie. Stifling a groan, he pictured their reactions.

Masterson followed his thoughts. "It's going to be tough on those girls. Some folks will blame them. Say they cornered him. We've got some narrow-minded people that are tight with the Baldwins."

"You're right." Joe grabbed his coat. "I'll fill them in before this hits the news."

"And they're likely to blame themselves, Chief. Second-guess their choices."

Angered by the senselessness, Joe thought of Matthew's poignant verse. "*For what profit is it to a man if he gains the whole world, and lose his own soul? Or what will a man give in exchange for his soul*?" Tom had traded poorly. Those left behind would sweep up pieces for years.

Ava's reaction mirrored Joe's. A hand shot to her mouth, distressed at Tom's choice. "God rest his soul. That poor family. Jeannine. Those children." Anguish twisted her normally regal features.

John didn't look nearly so bothered. Joe read his emotions, but didn't have the luxury of reflecting them. There'd be enough clean up to do in the coming days, weeks and months, that he couldn't afford to be happy that a lying, controlling, pedophile just offered up his soul. Mostly because it didn't seem like punishment enough.

"Is Anne up?" His voice subdued, Joe drew his mother's attention away from the band of hunters.

She started to comment, then read his face. "What's wrong?"

"Get her. Please."

Joe's father strode in, geared for a day in the woods. Seeing Joe, he stopped. "What's happened?"

Anne appeared in the doorway that separated the rooms, with Deb just behind. Her glance flitted from Joe to his father, then back. "Joe?"

There was no easy way to say this. "Tom Baldwin hung himself."

Anne's initial reaction was not what he expected. "That chicken-livered, no good—"

"Anne." Deb reached out an arm, her eyes sliding right.

Kyle stood there, sleepy, his forehead furrowed. "What's wrong?"

Joe scooped him up. "Nothing, Bud. Mommy's a little grumpy in the mornings."

"She is?" Kyle turned quizzical eyes to his mother.

Joe shrugged. "Well, she used to be. Until she went for her morning run, you couldn't talk to her."

"She's grown up since then," retorted Anne, her eyes mutinous. "Joe, how could he do that? Leaving Jeannine and those kids to deal with everything. I'd like to—"

"Let me take you to work." Keeping his voice calm, Joe noogied Kyle's head. Then he switched his look to Anne as another thought struck him. "Can you work today? Will you be okay?"

"Oh, I can work, all right," she sputtered, gathering her lunch and water, thrusting both into her tote. Her heated voice drew looks from the hunters. "I'd better work. Otherwise I'll think of how he denied us the satisfaction of seeing him squirm, watching him sweat."

She snapped the words. Joe leaned Kyle toward her. "Kiss Kyle good-bye. Mom will do breakfast for him. I've got the cruiser running."

She must have seen the sensibility of his plan. With a grim nod, she kissed Kyle's cheek and moved to the door, her expression dark. Jim McIntyre caught her arm, then pulled her in for a long hug. Holding her, he kept his voice low. "Personally, I don't mind that you won't have to sit in a room full of strangers and bare your soul, Annie."

She blinked back angry tears. Joe's heart broke at the sight, at the power Tom wielded from the grave. He wanted to damn him, then realized Tom Baldwin had saved him the trouble.

Right now a very big part of him hoped he had.

Newspaper headlines sprouted. In high school running, Tom Baldwin had been a force to reckon with.

He'd taught at elite running camps throughout the Northeast, and news of his humiliation and demise sent tongues wagging.

And on every tongue that pondered the improbability of a good man like Tom Baldwin taking advantage of a young girl, the names Kellwyn and Ellers were spoken with a touch of wondering suspicion.

CHAPTER TWENTY-TWO

No way could Anne stay.

She thought she could, at first. Joe's assurances and his parents' support smoothed the way through the initial aftermath of Tom's suicide. The funeral, the news reports, the angry words and assertions that followed.

"It'll die down," Joe had soothed her. "Give it time."

But when the Redmond principal revealed that four parents pulled their kids from school because they didn't want them exposed to adult topics, Anne knew she had to go. She'd been responsible for too much heartache over too many years. First Joe, then her mother. Now Tom's family, his runners, all grieving the loss of someone they loved and admired. Redmond would suffer loss of tuition because people didn't want innocent children corrupted by the talk surrounding her.

She was a pariah, marked and scorned. Well. Hadn't she known it would come to that eventually? That it *should* come to that?

Payback. Atonement. Reparation.

"Don't let intolerant people chart your path, Anne," Deb advised. "You did the right thing. Tom made the choice to kill himself. No one forced his hand."

Anne knew better. And when she received a threatening letter targeting Kyle, she knew her time was up.

"What do you mean, you want to move back to the house?" Joe asked, instantly guarded.

"It makes sense," Anne insisted. "Your parents have been wonderful, but it's time for them to get back to their normal routine. Same for me."

Joe took a step closer. "You're scared."

Her hesitation confirmed his suspicion. He grasped her shoulders. "I won't let anything happen to you. I promise. You don't need to run, Anne."

The sincerity of his words weakened her resolve, but then she thought of Kyle. "You can't be with us twenty-four/seven, Joe. And the thought that someone might mean Kyle harm has me tied in knots."

"In time," he began, but Anne interrupted him.

"My time's run out." She moved toward the window, wishing things were different. "Redmond has lost four students because of me, and there may be more."

"People's choices aren't your fault, Annie."

She turned back to him, appreciative but resigned. "Not my fault, but still my responsibility." When he started to protest, she raised a hand. "I can't take that on my shoulders, Joe. That a beautiful place like Redmond can't function because parents don't want their kids touched by unnecessary scandal. Can you blame them?"

The phone interrupted their conversation. Joe picked it up, then handed it to her. "Steve Clemmons for you."

From the school board? Puzzled, Anne accepted the phone. "Yes, Mr. Clemmons?"

"Ms. Kellwyn, we have a problem at the high school."

"Concerning me?"

"Yes. It seems our indoor track teams are refusing to run, jump or throw unless you take over as their coach."

"Their coach?" A surge of adrenalin revved her heart rate. "That's impossible. You know that, right? What would people think if I stepped into Tom's shoes? How would they react?"

"Exactly what the Athletic Director and I pointed out today, but the teams are insistent."

Anne grasped at practicalities. "Kids don't choose coaches. They take what they get and like it. Bill Heinrich can step up to the plate. He's helped Tom for years."

"Unfortunately the kids realize that Bill's a great guy and a lousy coach. They want you."

"But that's not possible."

"Which is why I'm calling," he agreed. "I need you to tell them that. Explain why it wouldn't be in anyone's best interests. With no evidence of wrong-doing on Tom's part, Forest Hills is suffering severe repercussions from this nasty business."

Whoa. Major red flags sprouted in Anne's brain.

No evidence? Did she hear right? "Mr. Clemmons, are you doubting the veracity of my allegations? And those of Jackie Ellers?"

"Ms. Kellwyn, my job is to keep an open mind until the facts are in. I'm sure you can appreciate the delicate balance a school board must maintain."

She didn't and said so. "Your delicate balance should err on the side of your students. Our charges against Tom Baldwin should make you more vigilant, not more defensive."

"A vigilance we demonstrated by relieving Tom of his duties once the charges were made public," Mr. Clemmons reminded her. "Ms. Kellwyn, can I count on your help? Will you address the runners and explain the unfeasibility of the situation?"

For a split second, Anne almost said yes. It made sense, after all. Why on earth would she consider putting herself in that predicament?

Because fifteen years is punishment enough.

No, the idea was ludicrous. Wasn't she just considering leaving, heading out?

If you run, he wins.

Joe's words, and accurate ones.

A choice faced her, an alternative, offering her options. Yes, there would be repercussions if she stayed. And more if she were to entertain the crazy notion of coaching Tom's team.

Correction: Forest Hills's team.

But running away brought repercussions as well. Fear. Disappointment. Longing. Defeat.

Still, could she stay here, knowing people's anger, possibly endangering Kyle?

She eyed Joe across the room, his eyebrow thrust up that she would consider such a thing. Hadn't she just reminded him that his protection was limited?

But mine is ever-present. Trust, daughter. Reach out.

Anne sucked a breath. "Mr. Clemmons, I'd like the board to consider my application for the head coaching position for indoor track and field. Since applications are available online, I'll download one, fill it out with the required references, and turn it in tomorrow. When is the next board meeting?"

His voice dragged, reluctant. Obviously he hadn't anticipated this possibility. Well, that made two of them. "Next Tuesday."

"I'll be there."

"You're kidding, right?" Joe approached her, worry lines etching his features. "You just wanted to make him squirm, correct?"

Anne shook her head. "Nope."

"But—"

"I'm sick to death of making decisions to please other people."

"So you'll make the one decision that enrages a populace and put yourself in danger?"

"I'm already in danger."

"More danger." He stepped forward, angry, his eyes dark with frustration.

"Then keep me safe."

"It's that easy?"

She slanted him a smile. "I do remember someone offering protection just moments ago."

"In-your-face moves up the stakes, Anne."

"So, up the ammo, Chief." She headed toward the dining room. The last week of deer season kept the lodge full, and Anne partnered with Deb for dinners. "I've got to get the dining room ready for supper. You can help, if you'd like."

"We're not done with this conversation," he warned. "This isn't a good move."

"It's the only move," she replied. She handed Joe a stack of bowls. "I'm tired of running, tired of hiding, Joe. You've said as much yourself. There's no honor in that."

"There's little honor in becoming someone's target, either," he retorted, setting bowls around with a distinct thump.

"Joe the bowls go on the sideboard, where the soup will be, so the guys can serve themselves family-style. Sheesh."

Why wasn't this bothering her? Probably because he was bothered enough for both of them. He moved closer, concerned. "So after fifteen years of silence, you're ready to take on the world in a matter of weeks? Pretty fast time frame."

Enjoying his proximity, Anne grazed a hand across his cheek, marveling at the feel of his skin, his late-day beard nubbing her fingers, and nodded. "There was no way I could have faced all this back then." She frowned, remembering. "I wasn't at the right place spiritually or emotionally. When I left you," she explained, raising her eyes to meet his, "I was a basket case. I hated Tom, I hated running, I resented my mother for not protecting me. I was irrational. Most of all I hated myself. I couldn't get beyond what I'd done. Instead of getting better, everything got worse." She shrugged. "Tom's letters tipped the scales so I ran."

"And me, Anne?" Joe's voice deepened. He closed the small distance between them. "Did you hate me for not shielding you? For not seeing what you were going through? Recognizing the problem?"

She tilted her head, remembering. "Oh, no, Joe." She kept it simple. "I loved you. You were..." A tiny frown wrinkled her forehead while a smile tugged her lips. "My husband. My lover. The strength I sought and needed. But I was so afraid I'd drag you down that I couldn't see a way out. Everything had gone dark. My faith was gone and I'd been living a lie for years. I felt like I brought nothing to our marriage, like I had nothing to give you."

"Annie." He crowded her space, invading her senses with his touch, his scent. She ducked her head to hide the raw emotion in her eyes, the longing. The love. "You had everything. You were all I ever wanted. Needed." There was a slight pause that seemed to linger forever. "Still are."

Anne brought her head up. Quick tears wet her eyes. "Joe..."

He set down the bowls with a clatter, and picked up a pile of napkins like it was any old day. Matter-of-fact, he placed the white squares at each place setting. "I need you, Anne. I need our life together. You were meant for me all along, and I knew it then. I was just too stupid to swallow my pride and come after you."

She watched him slide paper napkins under the edge of each plate. He looked up. "What are you thinking?"

"That this is a really strange way to have this conversation. Shouldn't we be," once more she chewed her lip, then glanced from his hands to his mouth, "kissing or something?"

"No."

"No?" Her hand paused, mid-air, holding a coffee mug. No little-handled cups at McIntyre's North Country Lodge. No, sir. Big, sturdy ironstone mugs, all the way. Joe set napkins until he stood in front of her again. Reaching out, he slipped the coffee mug from her hand before she dropped it and placed strong hands on her shoulders. Blinking, she searched his gaze. "You don't want to kiss me, Joe?" Uncertainty edged her voice.

He smiled a lazy smile, then slid his hands up, cradling her head. "Oh, I want to. I'm afraid I won't want to stop."

She shivered at his look, his words, her hands clutching his elbows.

"But I'm willing to risk it," he murmured as he brought his mouth to hers.

Like coming home. His touch, his mouth. The scent of wool and spiced cologne. The chill of his buttons under her fingers. "Joe."

"Talk later." His voice held amusement as his mouth resettled. "Right now I'm traveling down memory lane and thoroughly enjoying the trip."

She giggled and felt his mouth curve into a smile against hers.

"Marry me. Again."

"What?" She stepped back, amazed.

"Wrong answer." He followed, reclaiming her.

"Joe, are you sure?" Again she moved back.

"Reasonably certain." The note of humor in his voice notched up as he followed her movement once more. She went to back up another step. He grasped her arms. "You can back away all you want, but this time I'll follow, no matter how far or how long. Got it?"

Her heart felt huge. She saw the look in his bright, blue eyes. Warmth. Compassion. Sincerity.

Love.

With sudden clarity, every reason in the world why Joe shouldn't love her flooded back. Lies. Deceit. Promiscuity. Thoughts racked her as Joe's blue eyes searched hers. Shaking his head, he cocooned her in the shelter of his arms. "Don't do this to yourself."

She couldn't answer. Thoughts jumbled. She wasn't worthy of this man, of his goodness. Who was she kidding? If he knew—

Joe pulled back and tipped her chin. He met her gaze, then scraped a gentle kiss to her mouth, her forehead. "We both made mistakes." His voice reassured. The hand at her back rubbed in rhythmic, soothing fashion. "But it was a long time ago. Let's leave it there, okay?"

Once again his eyes met hers, his look steadfast and true. A part of her wanted to melt into that look, take the step forward to a life with Joe McIntyre.

Her fearful side needed to get away. Duck her chin and scurry under the nearest rock.

Reach out, daughter.

Anne drew a deep breath. Standing before her was a choice for the future, a chance to begin anew. But could she move away from the past that shadowed her for so long?

> ***I have swept away your offenses like a cloud, your sins like the morning mist. Return to me, for I have redeemed you.***

Isaiah's words flooded her. Joe stood, staid and quiet, one arm firm around her waist, the other hand cradling her cheek.

Reach out.

Could she? He was here, right here, offering her everything she'd thrown away. His heart, his home.

Did she deserve it?

Yes. Yes, if she believed God's word, His beloved redemption. Her sins may have been scarlet, but they were washed clean in Christ's love. Like wool, as white as snow.

Her right hand fingered the hem of Joe's woolen jacket. Leaning forward, she laid her cheek against the woven worsted, feeling like she'd come home.

Peace be with you. My peace, I give to you.

Woven wool, crisp air and rugged man scents swirled around her, her senses awakened. She wrinkled her nose and rubbed her cheek against his chest. "You smell good, Officer."

"Do I, Annie?" Hope tinged his voice.

"Oh, yes."

He gave her a little shake, then took a step back, eyeing her. "I'm still waiting for an answer and my good humor is diminishing in rapid fashion."

She grinned up at him, feeling lighthearted. Girlish. "You didn't ask a question, Joe. You made a demand."

"Big deal. Say yes." He grinned back at her, his eyes crinkled, his voice deep. Husky.

"Yes."

He looked surprised. "Really?"

She laughed out loud. "Really, truly. Do I get to live in the A-frame?"

His smile softened. The look in his eyes went warm and serious. "I built it for you. For our kids. Do you want more kids?" he asked suddenly, furrowing his brow.

"Kyle needs brothers and sisters," she assured him, letting her fingers touch the clean-cut planes of his face. "Lots of them."

His smile deepened. "I'd be happy to oblige the boy."

She shook her head at his arrogance. "Such an obligation on your part, Joe Michael."

His attempt to look humble failed. "I do what I can."

The thought of Joe, of their children, brought heat into her face. Joe stroked a cool finger to her hot cheek and gave her a knowing smile that put her in mind of long, sweet nights. "Are you blushing?"

She laid her cheek against the cool weave of his uniform once more. "Most likely. You have that effect on me."

"Good."

A movement from the kitchen brought them back to earth. Deb stepped in, both pleased and practical. "If you're done proposing, we really need to get supper finished."

Joe laughed. Anne dipped her head, embarrassed, then laughed with him. "Did you listen to the whole thing?" Joe kept his arms wrapped around Anne as his mother bustled around the room wearing a Cheshire cat smile.

"Of course. It was one of the best proposals I've heard. Good job, son."

"Thanks, I think." He loosed Anne, then eyed her hands. "I didn't come prepared to do this." His voice held a note of regret. "I don't have a ring."

Anne backed away. "Luckily, I do."

She returned with a jeweler's box and handed it to Joe. He snapped it open and eyed the diamond. "You didn't pawn this?"

She batted his arm. "No. What are you thinking?"

"You didn't like me all that much, Annie. I wouldn't have minded buying you a new ring."

"And you're perfectly welcome to do so." She laughed, holding out her left hand. "I'd like a mother's ring someday. One we can add birthstones to on a regular basis."

Joe slipped the diamond onto the hand it had known years before. "Still fits."

"Oh, yeah. It was meant for me." She waggled her fingers, watching the light dance against the pear-shaped stone. "Joe, I—"

"Nope. No more conversation. One more kiss then we help Mom with supper. Later we can make plans. Quick plans." His look was ripe with meaning.

Anne nodded in full agreement. "Yes."

CHAPTER TWENTY-THREE

"Anne's considering coaching the Forest Hills team," Joe told Boog the next morning.

"Like painting a target on her back," Boog replied.

"Don't I know it?" Joe frowned, dismayed. "I tried to talk her out of it."

"She wants to coach that bad?"

"She wants to stop running that bad."

Boog paused, considering. "Then that's a different story, Chief."

"Don't take her part," Joe warned. "You know this is a bad idea."

"I know it *could* be a bad idea," corrected Boog. "It also could be a great experience for all concerned."

"If we can keep her alive," grumbled Joe.

Boog grinned. "Somehow I think you'll manage it."

Joe left Boog's unsatisfied. Was he the only one that saw the rampant danger in Anne's choice?

Of course she'd like the opportunity to coach, and it was nothing that should be denied her. He'd seen her skills, and knew she had what it took.

But not Forest Hills. Dear Father in heaven, anywhere but there.

"We've got nothing except the statements of two young women and photos of a thirteen-year-old." Disappointed, Masterson reviewed the case with Joe.

"There's no photographic equipment, no cache of pictures, no hidden scrapbooks. We scoured Tom's office, his home, his car and his boat. We know he befriended Adriana Wellinger before she moved away, but it never went farther. The fact that he made her feel 'creepy', doesn't bear weight."

"Could the evidence have burned with the cabin?" Joe asked.

Masterson scowled. "Could have. Hard to say." His lips formed a thin line. After a short pause, he raised his gaze to Joe's. "I don't have the authorization to drag an investigation on with the perp dead. I would just like it settled for my own peace of mind. Tom's got a brother who isn't quick to forgive."

Rick Westbrook walked in. He nodded to Masterson and addressed Joe. "Afternoon, Chief."

Joe eyed him. "Didn't your brother Pete hang out with Tom and his hunting buddies now and then?"

Rick nodded. "Back in the day, yeah. They would hunt the upper ridge and move out from there. Why?"

Joe glanced at Masterson, saw his quiet assent. "We're looking for personal effects Tom may have stashed. Our thought was the cabin, but with that gone our evidence may have gone with it. Want to ask Pete if he knows of any hangouts we might have missed?"

"Wouldn't Baldwin have destroyed evidence once Jackie fingered him?"

Masterson answered. "Some would, but I don't think that's his profile. With his suicide, I'm sure he realized that the girls would miss their opportunity to punish him. Once again he foiled them, only this time it was from the grave. Unless he unloaded the pictures in his fireplace at home, they still exist. We know he didn't dump them in the trash or haul them out."

"You were watching."

"Yes."

Thoughtful, Rick reached for the phone. A short minute later he was connected to his older brother. “Pete. It’s Rick. Hey, back when you hunted with Tom Baldwin, did you guys hang anywhere besides the old cabin?” Listening, his expression went slack. He nodded. “Yeah. Got it. Sure. I’ll call. Set it up.”

Returning the phone, he shook his head. “Pete said they always originated or ended their hunts there. Sometimes they’d camp out in the cabin, other times they’d go home for the night and meet up first thing in the morning.”

Masterson didn’t look happy. Joe understood. Evidence would be a wonderful thing to have, something solid to back up Jackie and Anne.

The phone rang. Reaching forward, Joe answered it. Nodding, he handed it to Rick. “Pete.”

Surprised, Rick accepted the phone. “Hey, bro. What’s up?” Joe watched as Rick’s face went from constrained to hopeful. “In the creek bank?”

Masterson and Joe exchanged looks.

“Yeah, I’ve got it. Thanks, Pete.” Rick turned. “The old cabin had a root cellar. Pete says Tom’s dad fixed up the place while his cousin lived there after a messy divorce. Once he was gone, the cabin sat empty except for hunting season. But he says Tom mentioned the root cellar more than once, like he was familiar with it.”

Joe looked at Masterson. “Your search warrant covers it.”

Masterson eyed his watch. “Not enough daylight today. First thing tomorrow.” He stood and stretched out a hand to Rick. “Regardless of how it turns out, it’s worth checking.”

“Pete says there’s a door set in the creek bank that leads into the cellar, but it’s covered with vines and grass. There’s also a trapdoor in the floor of what had been the kitchen, but he didn’t know if it had steps or used a rope ladder.”

"I'll bring a fire ladder. One way or another, we'll check it out. Thanks, Rick."

The younger officer nodded. "It's all right.

CHAPTER TWENTY-FOUR

"You got that light, Chief?" Masterson's voice sounded unnaturally constrained as he stepped down the rungs of the fire ladder.

"Right here." Joe recognized the trepidation in the other man's tone. He gave the detective a look of understanding as he handed off the high-intensity flashlight. "Snakes or spiders?"

Masterson grunted. "Snakes. Always hated 'em."

"You see any?"

"No."

"I could arrange for some. Kyle likes to catch them."

"Stupid kid."

Joe laughed as Gina Rooks nudged his shoulder, rolling her eyes. Then they both went silent at Masterson's quick intake of breath. "Get down here."

Joe allowed Gina to go before him, then followed.

Paydirt.

Masterson's torch illuminated a squared-off room, finished off with painted concrete block and a poured cement floor. A generator stood in the corner, covered in dust. A small separate room was fixed with a single, dark bulb. Old-school photographic trays sat on the shelf, clean but dusty, not far from a more modern photo-friendly printer.

Masterson handed Joe the light. "See if that door works," he ordered, striding to a metal business desk that sat like a behemoth in a corner of the concrete cube.

Gina snapped pictures. The evidence techs would come through later, but they'd learned the hard way never to take anything for granted.

"Suicide was too good for him."

Both Gina and Joe turned. Masterson's tone seared more than the actual words. Joe stepped forward. Masterson held up a hand of warning. "You don't want to see these, Chief."

Joe paused, mid-step. Gina darted a glance from him to Masterson and back. Masterson's jaw worked as he flipped through a photo album, dated and noted. His language should have colored Gina's face, but it didn't. She stood calmly, watching him flick the pages with the edge of a pen.

While Masterson surveyed the evidence, Joe turned and pushed open the outside door with a mighty shove.

Light angled a narrow swath through the room as the myrtle vines gave way. Stepping out, Joe took in a deep breath of fresh air, pushing from his mind what they'd just discovered.

Digging Tom up to thrash him would do no good. Joe could only hope God meted out just punishment for a man who made a scrapbook out of defiling young girls. He walked to the hill's edge and stared at the creek, the northern banks coated with frost.

Footsteps approached from behind. Joe didn't turn. Masterson clapped a hand on his arm. "I didn't mean to bark. I just don't see the point—"

Joe shook his head, his jaw grinding. "I don't need to see them, to see what he did to Anne. I've lived it, watched it tear her apart and didn't have a clue. But we've got irrefutable proof now, and that should be enough to silence people. Even Tom's brother."

"I've got to get an evidence crew here." Pulling out his cell phone, Masterson dialed. Joe stepped away, contemplating the creek below.

Dualities puzzled him. He'd always been a straight up kind of guy and expected that in return. The idea that Tom could fool so many for so long, seemed frightening in its simplicity.

Over the years Joe had learned that evil wasn't always complex. Sometimes it was quite simple, staring you in the face, readily disguised. Joe sucked in clean, cold North Country air and couldn't be unhappy that Tom Baldwin was dead, that they could lay the whole thing to rest. The girls would be vindicated, just as they should be. In time, most would forget. Move forward.

Except for Anne and Jackie. They could forge ahead, but nothing would change what had happened to two, trusting children who harbored little girl crushes on their beloved coach.

Don't let me dwell on this, Lord. Let me move on like Anne's managed to do. Let me focus on her and Kyle. Don't let Tom's evil pull me into the pit.

Masterson clapped a hand onto Joe's shoulder. He turned, raising a brow.

"Two things."

Joe nodded.

"First, there was a third section in the book."

Joe frowned. "Another victim?"

Masterson shook his head. "Intended. Tom's heart attack got in the way."

Joe narrowed his eyes, then uttered a groan. "Missy."

Masterson nodded. "He had her earmarked. Her name was already written on the divider."

"We need to see the Volmers," Joe asserted. "Make sure she's not another victim who hid the truth." Joe's anger surged anew for a man who plotted and planned such atrocities.

"You know them?"

"In Forest Hills? Everyone knows everyone." Joe eyed the detective, noting the look in his eye. Shadowed. Reluctant. "What was the second thing?"

Masterson hesitated, then dropped his gaze to the churning water. "He loved Anne."

"He what?" Joe took a step back, sure he heard wrong.

"There's a journal of sorts. Nothing formal, and some of the entries are smudged, but the meaning's clear, Chief. Tom kept trying to replace Anne once he lost her to you."

Joe felt sucker-punched. He took another step back. Masterson grabbed his sleeve, his look noting the creek bank. "Watch the edge."

"He threatened Anne. He frightened her, made her run." Joe's tone said the detective's words made no sense. Masterson gave a slow nod.

"If he couldn't have her, you couldn't either."

Gina approached from the other side. "It was a long time ago, Chief. Don't let it eat you."

Joe stared at her.

She nodded, her face grim. "You got the girl. You won. Don't let this information make you crazy."

"But if it weren't for me-"

"No." Gina put a hand on Joe's sleeve. She shook her head. "He seduced Anne years before you were on the scene. Your relationship with her pushed him over the edge, but that was his doing. Not yours."

Masterson cut in from Joe's right. "*He* waited for *her*, Chief. Not the other way around, remember?"

God, help me. Help me to understand, to move beyond this.

Tom loved Anne? Joe's mind spun, considering it. Lust. Terror and threats. Blackmail. That wasn't love. Not even close. Power-lust, maybe. Obsession.

No, love was what *he* felt for Anne. For Kyle. Joe stretched his fingers out, feeling the muscles unclench.

He gave the detectives a quick nod, determined to bury his feelings. He'd deal with them later, on his own.

I will never forsake you. I will not leave you orphaned. I will never forget my own.

A hint of peace fluttered through Joe's roiling mind as Isaiah's words came back to him. Okay, then. Not on his own. He and God would sort it out.

Gina was right. He'd been given a second chance. He had the girl and the beginnings of the family he'd longed for. No way was Tom going to cheat him out of that. Joe met her eye and gave her a quick nod. "Let's get to the Volmer's. Brad, can you hang here for the evidence crew? It might be easier on Missy if Gina's there."

Masterson nodded, eyeing him. Apparently he was satisfied with what he saw. "I'll be glad to, Chief." He angled his head toward the creek side door. "Despite what we found, I'm glad it's over. Indisputable."

Joe nodded agreement. "Me, too." He started to stride away, then turned. "What you read, in that journal?"

Masterson cocked a brow.

"It stays between us," Joe asserted. "There's no reason Anne should hear of it. I don't want her bearing that responsibility."

Masterson took no time to consider the request. He nodded. "I couldn't agree more."

As the Forest Hills school board came to order that night, the room filled to overflowing. They'd changed venues, moving to the larger auditorium.

The room held a mix. Proponents from both sides came to be heard, along with concerned parents and the idle curious. Anne stood with Joe in the back, a churn of feelings working within her. Once the board finished approving last month's minutes, they opened the floor to discussion.

One by one people approached the podium, signing in, ready to speak their minds.

The Baldwin contingent stayed notably absent.

That started its own whispered comment until Detective Masterson stepped to the microphone. In a dry, no-nonsense voice, he revealed that a collection of photographic evidence tying Tom Baldwin to the attacks on two separate female children had been discovered earlier that day. Citing Tom's death, he explained the psychological anomaly of a person who could live two such separate lives.

"But I assure you he did," the detective made clear as he finished up. "The photographic evidence was presented to his family earlier today. There is no doubt that Tom was a predator, picking his victims carefully, then utilizing forms of behavior control to keep them quiet. He was a power-hungry man, despite the face he showed the public."

Anne leaned into Joe's strength, listening. He'd explained the find to her. Now he stood strong and silent behind her, appropriately recusing himself from tonight's board vote because of their relationship.

Anne hated that people saw pictures of her like that. The thought was unnerving.

But she'd moved far beyond the girl she'd been fifteen years past, and was determined to keep it that way. The flashbacks were mild now, the fear dissipated. The feel of Joe's strength at her back, his arms wrapped around her middle, was warm. Blissful.

Masterson's report quieted the naysayers. Looks were exchanged. Some appeared puzzled and confused, while others looked downright angry.

But not at Anne, this time, or Jackie. At themselves. And Tom Baldwin.

A middle-aged man walked to the front of the room. Anne angled her head, watching him, his face familiar.

"My boy ran for Tom nearly twelve years ago," he stated. He passed a hand across his chin and frowned. "He was a freshman when Annie Kellwyn was a junior. For two years I watched her run like the devil was after her." He cleared his voice, his emotion palpable. "I believe now that he was. Miss Kellwyn?" His eyes searched the crowded room for her.

Anne raised a hand of acknowledgement, feeling Joe's fingers tighten, protective.

Anne nodded to him. "Yes, Mr. Henry?"

"I need to apologize to you. I thought a lot of Tom. He helped my boy learn to run. Gave him lots of encouragement. But I see now that some other things Cory came home with, ideas of women and such, probably came right from Tom. I figured then it was part of high school. Now, I wonder." The man fidgeted the collar of his worn work coat before he cleared his throat to continue.

"I came here to object to you taking Tom's place. Right now I'm praying you'll give it a shot. Help us get over this whole mess."

Anne nodded. "Thank you, sir."

Briggs Volmer walked to the mike. Anne felt Joe straighten. Giving his hand a reassuring squeeze, she leaned into him.

"A lot of us owe apologies to Anne Kellwyn and Jackie Ellers," Briggs began. His eyes, dark with emotion, roamed the crowd. Despite the winter chill outdoors, a sheen of sweat brightened his brow. His depth of feeling resonated in his ragged tone. The slight shake of his hands. "We saw what we wanted to see. What Tom wanted us to see. I taught with Tom years back, before I was hired in Potsdam. My kids have all gone through Forest Hills schools, and I've never had a problem we couldn't solve."

Briggs paused and swiped a faded cloth to his face, his brow. "Then Missy came along, showing so much promise and potential. Tom was ecstatic at the thought of working with her. All through seventh grade he urged me to let her run with the high school teams. He talked about the scholarships she could win, the help she'd get. He knew money was tight since..." His voice wavered. He drew a breath, then exhaled slowly. "Since we lost Missy's mother. He dangled the thought of that college money like you'd tempt a fish with a worm."

His tone grew choppy. The shaking of his hands rattled the paper he clutched. He shook his head as though arguing with someone, making a point. "I said no, at first. Missy's a great runner, but she wasn't old enough or mature enough to be hanging out with seventeen and eighteen year-old girls. There's a big difference in conversation from twelve to eighteen."

Heads nodded.

"But Tom kept urging me, saying her best shot at a scholarship was for him to get her young. Trainable."

Anne's heart clenched. Her throat constricted.

"Dear God, I had no idea what he meant." Silent tears welled, then spilled from the big man's eyes. Tears for not following his common sense, letting someone else plan the destiny of his children?

Or tears for the girls who hadn't gotten Missy's reprieve?

"I said yes in eighth grade as long as Tom promised to monitor her carefully. He laughed and said that's just what he had in mind. That he hadn't had a protégé like her since Kellwyn and Ellers."

The crowd gasped. Emotion clenched Anne's gut. The tears she'd controlled so far spilled over, slipping onto Joe's strong fingers. He tugged her closer, dropped his head to hers.

"Chief McIntyre and the sheriff's detectives came to see me today." Briggs Volmer's eyes sought them in the audience. He nodded in their direction and wiped his nose, unashamed. "They asked some pretty tough questions about Missy. They interviewed her.

Watching her, seeing her squirm, I couldn't bring myself to imagine what Anne and Jackie went through. First the attack from their coach, then the attack from their community. Who watches out for children these days if not their families, friends and neighbors?" He shook his head, swiping the cloth across the wetness of his face once again. "My daughter is safe, thank God, but only because Tom suffered a heart attack three days before the 'photo shoot' he'd scheduled with her."

The crowd went silent. Briggs nodded. "He told her he wanted shots to use for promotional purposes. Said it would help her be a better runner if he created a package like he did with Ellers and Kellwyn."

Briggs blew his nose on a wad of tissues a board member handed him. "Time and again Tom used double entendre and we were too trusting to see it. To realize what he was.

"But I saw my daughter's name in his photo album. A section made ready for Missy Volmer. Thank God her section never got used."

Raising his eyes, Briggs sought Anne and Joe with his look. "I would be honored to have Anne Kellwyn coach my daughter. Frankly, I can't imagine why she'd want the job after what's happened, but she could make a difference here. A big difference. That's all I have to say."

Stepping down, he wove his way through the crowd to Anne and Joe. Reaching out, he hugged Anne, then shook Joe's hand. "Thank you both."

Anne jutted her chin into the air, mustering a smile through damp eyes. "I'd love to coach Missy, Briggs. Either in school, or privately. Thank you."

"No." The look on the father's face at the thought of his daughter's narrow escape was telling. "I'm the one who's grateful. It took guts for you girls to come forward. Incredible guts. I'm only sorry people didn't get behind you sooner."

"Tom was good at what he did," Joe reminded them. "Anyone knowing his law-abiding side would reject the notion he could be so dark."

"Still." Briggs refused to excuse the town. "We need to protect our own. We didn't. It's time to face that and move on."

The athletic director called for attention. As the room quieted, he turned their way. "Ms. Kellwyn? Anne?"

"Yes?" Swiping her eyes one more time, Anne stepped forward.

"The Forest Hills Athletic Department, with full approval of the Forest Hills School Board, would like to offer you the head coaching position for the coming track and field season. You would be assisted by Bill Heinrich and Mary Hines. Will you accept this position, Anne? With our thanks and gratitude?"

Anne felt Joe's touch of reassurance to her shoulder. Glancing up, she saw the approval in his eyes. She turned back to the board and the athletic director. "On one condition."

"And that is?" Mr. Clemmons inclined his head.

"I won't use Tom Baldwin's office."

The board nodded as a group. No one had a problem understanding that. "We'll make arrangements for a different area," Mr. Clemmons promised. "Your space will be ready Monday afternoon."

Anne sucked a breath, then nodded in return. "I accept the position."

Slapping the gavel once more, the A.D. stepped around the table and made his way down the crowded center aisle. When he reached Anne, he extended a hand. "I'd like to be the first to thank you, tell you how much we appreciate this." His eyes and tone reflected his empathy for the situation. His gaze swept their surroundings, the familiar auditorium, the crowd of people dealing with news they would have a difficult time digesting. "Welcome home, Anne."

Anne clasped the hand, returning the firm grip with one of her own. Raising her chin, she wasn't sure whether to smile or cry. With a gentle touch from Joe, the smile won. She nodded again and met the man's gaze, eye to eye. "It's good to be back."

OTHER BOOKS BY RUTH LOGAN HERNE:

Independently Published:

Try, Try Again

From Love Inspired Books:

North Country:

Waiting Out the Storm
Made to Order Family
Winter's End

The Men of Allegany County Series:

Reunited Hearts
Small-town Hearts
Mended Hearts
Yuletide Hearts
A Family to Cherish
His Mistletoe Family

Kirkwood Lake Series:

The Lawman's Second Chance
Falling for the Lawman
The Lawman's Holiday Wish (December, 2013)
Loving the Lawman (May, 2014)

From Summerside Press:

*Love Finds You in the City at Christmas (October 2013)

*Two novellas featuring Ruth Logan Herne's "Red Kettle Christmas" and Anna Schmidt's "Manhattan Miracle"

BUY LINK : http://amzn.to/154pnGN

AUTHOR BIO

Born into poverty, Ruth Logan Herne likes to be called "Ruthy", she loves God, family, her country, chocolate, sweet coffee and dogs. Constantly surrounded by small children, she spends her daylight hours wiping noses and telling stories, then pens sweet books by candlelight in an inglenook fashioned just for her. Okay, that last part is probably NOT TRUE, but she does write in the middle of the night, while the dogs snore nearby. A mother of ~~six,~~ **SEVEN** children (she may or may not have stolen her sister's daughter at some point in time) she's a grandmother, a story-teller, a gardener whose specialty is weeds these days, and she sings in a delightful choir where they carefully overlook her limited abilities in the name of Christian charity. She is ever-grateful for that! E-mail Ruthy at ruthy@ruthloganherne.com or you can visit her at her website http://ruthloganherne.com, in Seekerville, www.seekerville.blogspot.com where she hangs with an absolutely lovely bunch of inspirational authors at the Yankee Belle Café www.yankeebellecafe.blogspot.com or at her blog Ruthy's Place www.ruthysplace.com. You can also find her on facebook, twitter and Goodreads!

Mount Laurel Library
100 Walt Whitman Avenue
Mount Laurel, NJ 08054-9539
856-234-7319
www.mountlaurellibrary.org

Made in the USA
Middletown, DE
15 February 2022

61148288R10142